BEN BRACKEN: ORIGINS

PRAISE FOR THE BEN BRACKEN STORIES

'...Bracken is the UK's answer to Jack Reacher..."

"Really enjoyed this. A compelling, heart-stopping thriller with a really interesting and provocative central character. I certainly want to see what Ben Bracken gets up to next. It makes a change to find a book in which the story is based in the UK (Manchester to be precise). I bought this for my holidays in Spain next week and just started to read it - then found I couldn't put it down and spent the entire spare time of the bank holiday reading it!"

"Intriguing read. It holds your interest very well. Is not a predictable book. I am sure you will love it."

"I've never quite read a story like Deansgate Deadline. I loved the darkness and mystery surrounding the main character, Ben Bracken. I hope to see more from this author, following Bracken's back story. There are lots of questions about this mysterious man that I'd love to have answered. This read was immediately intriguing"

THE DEANSGATE DEADLINE

1

It is the dead of night. The air is crisp, the sky a dirty blue, and the city of Manchester sleeps - a slumbering troll of granite, glass and humanity.

Trev walks across the quiet cobbles of the city's Northern Quarter, with his earphones jammed in and his collar up tight. He is on the happier side of 30 but at this early hour looks like an unsettling cocktail of insomnia and zombie. The Northern Quarter is Manchester's miniature New York city - part homage, part kiddy version. Trev likes it there and he crosses the road to his flat on Church Street. He uses the key fob to open the door, which responds immediately with a soft beep and the click of a lock somewhere.

He checks for post in the metal mail lockers opposite the door - this time more out of habit than anything. He knows there'd be no post at this unsociable hour. Along the hall from the lockers, he calls the lift, which was luckily already resting on the ground floor. It lets him in immediately. Inside, he selects the 5th floor and leans against the wall, letting out a deep sigh. He is, in regular speak, zonked. A long shift, barreled straight into a late night which thundered into almost an all-nighter, but he just managed to stem the flow of work long enough to get home, get a couple of hours shuteye before it all starts again in a couple of hours. The mere thought of it sends Trev a bit sickly.

The lift arrives on five, and he walks out, popping his earbuds out as he goes. He undoes his jacket, and jangles the keys from his jeans pocket, heading for flat 526. He reaches the door, and takes extra care when putting the key in the lock to ensure it's as quiet as he can possibly do it. The door opens with a clunk, which brings a slight grimace. All day, every day, noise carries itself around the building like an omnipresent rude landlord - always there, always making it's presence felt. He opens the door and goes inside.

The flat is usually pretty beautiful. High ceilings, expansive windows, hearty bare floorboards. But as he opens the door, it looks anything but. The shelves that line the entrance hallway have been ripped bare, with the contents all over the floor. Pictures smashed, books ripped, ornaments broken beyond recognition. Trev is immediately concerned and terrified, panic rising dizzily without rhyme or respect. He panics not for his things, but for the person who was here when he left yesterday.

'Freya!' he shouts, as he jumps over the debris on the floor and rounds the corner - to see the entirety of the flat's open living-space laid bare. It's been practically destroyed.

Even though the lights are off, he can see fine - thanks to the orange glow of the fridge that has been ripped from the wall and upended, it's contents spilling out onto the floor like innards on the Savannah next to a fresh kill. The rest of the room is almost an ode to the destruction of the hallway. Destruction all over the floor, debris everywhere. The coffee table is upended, the plasma tv has a crystalline hole in it and the sofa has been slashed. His Playstation sits on the kitchen counter, strangely nowhere near the tv, with a hammer embedded cruelly through it's plastic housing.

No time to stop, Trev pretty much surveys the damage on the move as he keeps following the arc of the hallway to the bedroom. He throws open the bedroom door, to the same level of disarray in his once (almost) immaculate bedroom.

'Freya!' he cries. 'Are you here?'

No answer again. He checks the ensuite - empty, and largely untouched by the mess. He checks the main bathroom just out in the main hallway, the last remaining room of the flat unchecked. Empty again, only the soap bottles and cleaning products around the sink have been smashed. He heads straight back into the living room.

He steps on the debris, crunching it down, while he scours the room to look for some sign of Freya, but he knows it's useless. Freya isn't here. Two thoughts begin to dominate Trev's mind and wage a war against each other for prominence: who would do this? and: where is Freya? Practicality begins to dawn and this causes a third thought to emerge: POLICE.

He goes to the wall mounted phone by the door, which is by some miracle still there. As Trev gets nearer, he realizes it's no miracle. Stuck onto the front of the phone, right across the keys, is a bright green PostIt note. On it, in marker pen, is scrawled:

0161694489 - DO CALL.

Trev looks at it hard, as if searching for a clue from the note as to who is behind the madness left here. Nothing. If anything, the handwriting is rather neat. He knows he has to call. He thumbs the number in, trying not to jitter the handset out of his hands.

He holds the phone to his ear and listens. Ringing. And again. And again. And again. Then:

'It is truly about time.' A voice greets.

'Who is this?' Trev murmurs.

'On the standard scale of one to ten, how do you like the remodel?' The voice is male, and has a scratchy depth to it that suggests middle age, perhaps older. The accent is cockney, all apples and pears.

'What do you want?' Trev pleads.

'Listen to this please' the voice asks. The line quietens, then a struggle can be heard. A muffled couple of thuds, the rustle of fabric, and the odd frightened squeek. Trev is distraught - he knows immediately who it is.

'Trev! Trev!' screams Freya. Her voice contains a timor that Trev has never heard before. Utter terror. Hearing it for the first time horrifies Trev. His protective instincts for Freya take a violent surge.

'Freya!' gasps Trev. 'Where are you!?'

The male voice returns, a little quieter, as if away from the phone. 'Tell him what you can see'.

'No' Freya retorts stubbornly.

More struggle, but it is stopped almost as soon as it has begun by a deeper thud.

'Tell him what you can see' the man repeats.

Trev can't take anymore, and tries to inject calm into his voice. 'Tell me, baby'.

'It's very dark. I'm in a room somewhere. I'm alone with this... man but his friends are just outside. He has a gun pointing at my forehead.'

Trev's world pretty much bottoms out. The man's voice taunts out, 'Where's my finger?'

'The trigger' Freya whispers.

The man's voice becomes louder, as he takes the phone.

'Right then , we have established your problem. Your problem is, your dolly-bird here is a twitch away from a bullet up her nose. That should prompt some kind of co-operation from yourself. I'm being rhetorical, you don't need to answer. You have a laptop, don't you?'

'I have a bunch of laptops' Trev responds. He works for PC Planet as part of the IT staff, and repairing computers is kind of his entire job description.

'Blue carbon lid, black base unit, 7.5 inch screen, 50 gig hard drive'.

'I have that laptop'. Trev remembered it because of how rubbish it was, and was amazed that anyone seriously wanted to repair a 200 quid laptop.

'That's my laptop - you bring it to me by 8am. What state do you think this bitch's face will be in by 8:01 if you don't?'

Trev doesn't speak. No words necessary really - it's pretty simple.

'I'll take that crushing silence as your complete compliance. I'm in 3298 Beetham Tower. I don't need to tell you where that it do I?'

'No.' Trev whispers. Of course he didn't. Beetham Tower is the solitary skyscraper that dominates the Manchester skyline, and, as Trev looks up from the phone to the windows, he can see Beetham Tower itself in the distance - right at the bottom of Deansgate, the road on the west of Manchester city centre which takes you from the top of the city to the bottom. Trev can see some of the lights in the skyscraper on, even at this hour, and he wonders which one is hosting the disastrous scene he can hear down the phone.

The phone goes dead, the dial tone drone almost mocking Trev's submission to the crisis.

He sits motionless. To Trev it feels like he is sitting in a crater of despair, his world around him an awful catastrophic mess, with himself a broken epicenter.

He eventually puts the phone down, if only to drown out the mess. Then he reaches for his bag. He knows the laptop is in there, and he knows the consequences if he boots it up. He wrestles with that and realizes he has no idea who he is dealing with. None at all.

He takes out the laptop, and it hits him: all this trouble for a rubbish little notebook. It was a piece of shit brand new, never mind now, he thinks. What could possibly be on there of such value? It's hard drive is absolutely paltry - it's not like you could even store anything of any note on there! Curiosity tugs and claws, and almost subconsciously, he finds himself pressing the power button.

Straight away, the screen flashes to life. The notebook had only been on sleep mode. The screen is dead - just blackness. Man, it really is busted, he thinks. He waits, in case it needs to boot up after all. After a moment, he notices the cursor, and he realizes: this is the desktop and it doesn't have a single icon on it. No picture, just a black background. He directs the cursor to the bottom, to bring up the start tab. Nothing.

He listens to the machine - sounds just fine, a familiar soft whirr. He just needs to get at the contents. He expertly enters the root file of the computer manual index, and boom, the doors open. There are things here, that's for sure. No programs, just a series of text documents.

It strikes Trev as clever - a hidden library masked on the premise of a broken computer. The text document files all have names - girls first names. Trev feels a quake in his guts - immediately, he doesn't like where this is going. He scrolls down a touch, and as he reads, sickness, revulsion, rage and horror blend a dangerous mix and swamp his thoughts.

As he previews the documents, he sees names, genders, dates of birth, locations and vital statistics. At first it seems like the world's most basic dating website, no pictures, just text. Then he sees each one has a price, with three currencies listed - pounds, euros, dollars. Now it resembles a seedy escort agency's online menu. Then he twigs the dates of birth, which rocks him to the core. The dates of birth are staggeringly recent. Really, jaw-droppingly recent. There are kids as young as three listed, and none older than twelve. The notebook represents a vile catalogue of paedophile sickness, a stomach-churning morass of the most immoral and base taboo. What Trev holds in his hand, appears to be the central nerve centre of a nationwide child sex ring.

Trev can't believe simple text could hit so hard. He yanks his mobile out of his pocket, and now knows there's only one number he can call. He thumbs through the contacts and stops on Ben Bracken.

2

The Campanile Hotel walls are peeling. A pastel lemon wallpaper that once might have been considered classy now looks worn and a bit sickly - it could well be the colour swatch for nausea. From his bed, Ben Bracken has to turn onto his stomach to avoid the sight of it. He is wide awake, but he shouldn't be. He drank enough to fell a silverback last night, but no amount of alcohol will send him to sleep. The drink is a big problem, but what makes it worse is surely the lack of sleep. He can't sleep off the epic hangovers he surely gives himself, so the following day is just another gross battle through a hangover until he gets to that next pint. But in this spiral he is in, it only starts the process again.

Alongside the bubbling hangover rests a deep bitterness, which has nestled in and buried itself down rather happily. It nags, tugs and pulls, but it never seems to make any effort to get out. And Ben doesn't do anything to rid the infestation either. He feeds it with the booze, and he knows it - but he also knows he isn't done wallowing yet. Plenty more where that came from.

He's only been back in the country 3 weeks (and 2 days), but he's already had enough. He saw more in the combat-torn dustbowl of Helmland Province to last a lifetime, and his perspective took a jarring he will never shake. He has seen things no man should ever see, felt things no man should ever feel and done things any man would wish he could take back. He knows the past is the past. Nothing can change who he is now.

He will never get over his exit from the armed forces, and the sense of betrayal is so palpable it burns with every breath. He will never understand the society he had given everything to protect - such sacrifice for a people and way of life he just doesn't get. He must have known it at the time, but it now simply doesn't compute. He sees persecution for the people that return from combat even when they left the army on the right terms - God knows what they make of Ben and his dishonourable discharge. Just another thing he must live with, that he can't do anything about.

The hate begins to well in him, that familiar swell of a hot red tide against the corners of his skull, and the vomit begins to rise with it. He reaches for the bin by the bed, strategically placed there the night before, when the phone rings. The sudden noise jars his combat-taut senses and prompts immediate action - he has answered the phone before he has even recognized it is ringing.

'Yes' he says.

'Ben, it's Trev here, are you up?' The familiar voice of his old schoolfriend Trevor Houghton should ease his state, but it doesn't - not at this hour.

'What's happening, Trev?'

'I have a big problem' Trev responds, his voice ragged.

'Go - all the details' Ben instructs.

'Freya has been kidnapped by some... really bad guys. I can't go to the police, they'll kill her.'

Ben is in the zone, hangover forgotten. The memory of problem-solving in violent situations pulls focus into clarity and it's a familiar one. It's something he is good at, and at this stage, it is welcome. Adrenaline hits his hangover for six - it'll come back later, but this crisis needs immediate attention.

'Do you have a location?' Ben asks.

'3298 Beetham Tower.'

'What do they want?'

'A laptop. It's filled with details of a child sex ring that the leader seems to operate.'

Ben is silent for a second in revulsion, but then he can only shake his head as two questions rattle angrily inside him - what society have I really come back to!? This is the society I gave everything to protect!?

'You have the laptop?'

'Yes'

'You have a deadline for its return?'

'8am.'

'You have a contact number for them?'

'Yes, it's-'

Ben interrupts. 'Save the rest for when I see you. Bring the laptop and the number to Castlefield, Canal Side opposite Dukes. I'm down at the Campanile, only 400 metres from Beetham Tower. As you come down, come through the side streets and through Spinningfields. They'll have eyes on Deansgate.'

'Will do. I'll set off now.'

'No, we have time. Get a black coffee, four spoons of the instant stuff you have. Take a second, compose yourself. The closer we leave it to deadline, the more things are in our favour. They are sex-traffickers, not killers - they'll be bricking it about maybe having to kill someone.'

'You're sure?'

'Yes.' Ben wasn't.

'OK.'

'It's 5.20 now. Meet me at 6.00 where we discussed.'

Ben hangs up, and immediately gets out of bed. He is still dressed in the black combats (once you get used to pockets everywhere, it seems stupid not to have them anymore) and the frayed red shirt (10 years old, one of the only 'going out' shirts he has) he wore the night before. He grabs his pack, army issue, camouflage covered, and opens it. His mind is so fixed on the objective, that he forgets to worry for his friend and the safety of Freya. It would be wasted energy - right now, it's fixing time.

3

A light mist hangs over the Manchester Ship Canal, as a couple of Greylag geese saunter around the bows of a moored barge. The scene would be idyllic, if it weren't for the grim tide raging inside Ben's mind. Nothing looks pretty when you feel like this. He looks up, to his left. Beetham Tower looks perilously close now, and stares down at him almost screaming 'come and have a go if you think you're hard enough!'. 3298, Ben thinks, over and over again.

He can hear footsteps from the bridge to his right, echoing through the stillness. Ben checks his watch - a reliable old school Casio - and thinks 'Right on time'.

Trev appears through the tunnel, walking briskly, with a backpack. He notices Ben, and marches straight to him, breaking into a slight jog as he approaches.

'Save it, save it,' Ben instructs, gesturing a slowing down motion with his hands.

'It's taken every part of me not to sprint all the way here' Trev replies.

'You alert?' Ben asks. He scrutinizes him carefully.

'Yes - wired to high hell.'

Ben eyes him. 'I'll tell you all sorts of sorry's about what's happened as soon as we get out of there,' he points over his shoulder to the hulking tower leaning over them. 'But now is certainly not the time'.

'What's the plan?' Trev asks.

'The laptop.' Ben holds his hand out.

Trev unshoulders the pack and a quick rummage brings out the notebook, he hands it over. Ben shuts his eyes on receipt.

'The kids...' Ben states grimly. 'Are they... young?'

Trev sighs. 'Yes, very.'

In one motion, Ben drops the laptop across his now-rising knee and splits the machine into fractures of plastic, metal, circuitry and motherboard.

'What the fuck are you doing?'

'Two things. One: I'm making them address us. How are they going to bargain with us if we don't have anything to bargain with? Two: I'm shutting down one sick kiddy sex ring. Step one is done.'

'How do you do step two?' Trev asks.

Ben points midway up Beetham Tower. 'By ripping the head off the serpent.'

'You boys are out early!' A voice cuts through the crystal air. It's female with a playful air that doesn't really fit the scene.

Both Ben and Trev snap around to the source, and standing near the tunnel entrance are two women, all leather, straps, PVC and heavy make up. Textbook prostitutes, Ben thinks.

'Not now, thank you,' calls Ben, preempting the come on.

'Oh, look at you, wandering about at this time, you're still dressed like you're looking for some action' the taller of the two shouts. In heels (massive ones) she is just over six feet, but six and a half with the beehive that sits merrily and messily up top. She takes a big stride over.

'We do look a little overdressed for jogging' suggests Trev.

'One each, how convenient! We can do you a special!' shouts the smaller one, who by normal standards, is not that small. Her eyelashes look like they could whip someone else's eye out, never mind her own. They are approaching, in an awkward mix of attempted sexiness while trying to cover the ground quickly to get to them. It doesn't look so bad on the smaller one, but the tall one looks like a horny giraffe at pub closing time.

'Did you see them as you arrived?' Ben murmurs softly to Trev.

'No.'

'You recognize them at all?'

'Never seen them.'

'OK.' Ben steps forward, gaining a physical rebuff to their advancement. It always amazed Ben how animal human interaction can be, no matter the circumstances. It didn't slow the oncoming women at all, but that gives Ben all the info he needs. There is another purpose to their being here, and it's not to close the deal on one last trick for the night.

As they get to the men, there is a slight slowing, as they fork and each pick a man to approach. The tall one goes for Ben, the smaller one angles for Trev. Ben steps quickly centrally to block them both off.

'Ladies, I did say, now is not the time.'

Ben feels the whistling knife before he even sees it. The tall one is bringing her right hand up from her side to Ben's neck at slashing speed. Ben was expecting it, and takes an angled step forward to meet it, bobbing right to avoid the knife and blocking with his left arm. As he blocks the knife-arm, he dips low and lets rip a furious uppercut into the woman's guts, damn near doubling her up over his fist.

He almost has to shake her off his hand, as the little one dives and claws at his head and shoulders. It reminds Ben of when he was a kid growing up in Yorkshire, when the family cat would get a bit rowdy and have a bit of a pop at you. He grabs hair, and yanks. Part of the hair comes away, a horrible cheap weave, but the hair that is firmly attached, he holds on to. He pulls the woman off him and holds her at arms length - and plants a vicious headbutt right on the bridge of her nose. Her caterwauling cuts instantly and she hits the cobbles like a sack of manure. The other woman gasps for breath, and Ben can only spit words at her.

'If you know what's good for you, you'll shut up.'

The breathing softens. It all took place in about 4 seconds. Trev stands there amazed, unmoving.

'You... hit a woman.'

'No, I hit two women. Trev - if someone's trying to chiv your throat out take them down by any means. If you really have to, check for meat and two veg afterwards.'

Trev has absolutely no comeback for that one. 'Were they....?

'Yes - they must have been following you. It's when they saw that you weren't alone they acted.'

'Jesus' Trev looks at the two women on the floor. 'I haven't seen anything like that before.'

'I dare say it'll get worse than that before we hit deadline. Now let's go. Follow me. We are going through the hotel, but the flat number you gave me is up in residential.'

The two men start to jog towards the tower, leaving the two prone women on the floor. A goose honks solemnly in the distance - a foghorn for the stormy times ahead, Trev thinks.

4

The lobby is a cavern of marble, glass and titanium, but at this time, there is also silence. A lone receptionist sits at the check-in desks on the left, with an even lonelier security guard by the revolving doors. There would have been activity more earlier, but at 6.40am? The drunks have long gone home, and the day is getting started - or at least it would be, but it's a Sunday, and therefore even quieter than normal.

Ben marches straight in, nodding an acknowledgement to the guard. Best way to gain acceptance somewhere is to act like you are supposed to be there, Ben thinks. He arrows to the desk, with the same sense of purpose that gives the guard no reason to worry or assume the worst, and approaches. Trev follows him closely, still carrying a very empty looking backpack.

Ben knows, from his life prior to the armed forces, that there are few things in life worse than a night shift, and there are few things in life better than a quick buck. As he walks he takes a fifty pound note out of his pocket, and as he gets to the receptionist, he drops it on the counter. The receptionist is a rather quiet looking bloke who looks like it is taking every ounce of energy not to slump off his chair with exhaustion.

'I need to get up to residential, fast and quiet', he states, matter-of-factly. His tone stinks of 'don't ask'. The receptionist doesn't. A moment of indecision passes, before he reaches for the note. 'We're in', thinks Ben. 'How the hell is he doing this?' thinks Trev.

The receptionist whisks the note into his blazer pocket and stands, and as he does so he simply utters 'This way.'

He points to the lift block to the right of the desks, and Ben and Trev head towards the recess. The receptionist points into the back wall of the area that houses the lifts, to the wood panels that line the doors. One of the panels has a key hole. Taking a keyring from his trouser pocket, that appears to have a good 20 keys on it, the receptionist selects a key and opens the door. As it swings open, motion activated lights blink on beyond to reveal a cold grey concrete stairwell. Ben and Trev enter, and the receptionist immediately closes the door behind them.

Again, it has all happened so fast. Or it least, it had for Trev. Ben was actually a little disappointed they were in the lobby as long as they were, fearing anyone could have seen them. But still, he knows it hasn't exactly gone badly.

Trev looks up the stairway, and sees what looks like hundreds of floors stacked up above of them. Ben starts walking the stairs steadily.

'Walk, don't run.' instructs Ben. '30 second breaks every five floors. Don't want to risk burnout.'

'Of course.' Trev responds, and falls into place at Ben's side like an obedient dog.

They traverse the stairs at a steady pace. As they climb, Ben's thoughts rattle to possibilities and planning, while counting the floors. 'Assess number of hostiles...13... Locate hostiles... Find best exit... 14... Locate Freya... Get hands on firearm... 15... Keep Trev safe... Find the main man... 16...'

His thoughts pop in at random, but they meld onto each other to form a cogent map in his head with a plan of detailed instructions alongside it. He always adhered to the notion that a good plan is better than any weapon you may be carrying... but he also firmly believes that it's better to have a gun and not need it than need a gun and not have it. And at this present moment he is very short of firepower. He knows, that if they are packing up there, he has to get his hands on a firearm to even the odds.

It's different in England. A lot different to Afghanistan, and before that, Iraq. He knows that nobody is supposed to have a gun here, and the penalty for carrying illegally is severe. That has always been somewhat of an under-rated deterrent, but he doesn't quite know what he is dealing with here. They may be armed to the teeth, but they may only be armed with bad intentions and nothing else. Who knows. If he prepares for the worst, however, anything better is a pleasant bonus.

They edge ever closer to 32, and like a marathon pacesetter, Ben has to mentally drag Trev up the last few flights. As they get to 32, they stop. Ben takes a moment to let Trev catch his breath, while inching open the door to take a look. It's a deserted hallway, with colorful carpets and smart looking mood-lighting. Ben creaks the door open a touch more, to see the number on the nearest front door. 3267. They are close. He closes the door.

He hunches to Trev's level, while Trev struggles to take his head from between his knees.

'Trev, you wait here. Doesn't matter what you hear. Stay here. When I step outside the next person who uses that door will be Freya. Take Freya and go down. Do not wait. As soon as you see her, you grab her and go. No excuses. You go.'

'There's nothing I can say about this is there?' Trev wheezes.

'Nothing at all' Ben responds. 'You won't see me again till it's over. I'll find you on the outside sometime.'

'Thank you' Trev looks at him earnestly.

Ben stares back. It's the first time anyone has thanked him for any sacrifice he has made, for any effort he has put in under the most extreme pressure. It catches him cold, and he can only nod back. Without a word, he turns back to the door.

He cracks it open again, just a touch, and sees the hallway is still empty. He checks his watch - 7.07. Pretty good timing, thinks Ben. Close enough to jitter the enemy, but with plenty of time to assess and take a cooler approach. He opens the door fully and enters the hallway. As he slowly eases the door shut behind him, he catches Trev lowering himself onto the step. Ben was once like that - subservient to the situation around him. He turns to the hall and begins to move.

He checks the door numbers and watches them tick upwards as he passes them.   The place really is quiet, which is to be expected. But they must know that someone is coming. They are not expecting him though - that's why Trev is firmly hidden, way out of sight.

The hallway ends at a T-junction, and as Ben approaches it, he gravitates to the left hand wall. He doesn't know whether to go left or right, but as he edges his head around the corner to see, he knows he has to go left straight away - because the third door on the left has a tall man standing next to it. The welcoming committee, thinks Ben.

Immediately Ben has him pegged from his posture - about 210 pounds, pretty well-built, but that 210 is spread across a 6'4" frame. And it's spread pretty thin.

He is about 40, with a completely skewed nose that suggests he's not scared of a scrap or two. He hunches, and his back looks a little arched. He's been standing there a while. He wears jeans, a white shirt and a blazer - he looks like an awkward uncle desperately trying to fit in at your 18th birthday party.

Ben turns and faces just where he came from, cups his hands around his mouth and begins to whistle. He can't think of particular song to whistle, so he starts with 'Somewhere Over The Rainbow'. He slowly turns round to the corner, throwing the whistle from further down the corridor back to where he was stood, mimicking an approach. As he turns to face the corner, he lowers his hands and starts to walk briskly around into the left hand corridor. He sticks his left hand in his pocket and feigns a good rummage.

The guard looks up immediately, but Ben keeps his head down. As he walks, he keeps the whistle up. He pulls out his old house keys - he still carries them, a memento of his past and a reminder that he once had a place to call home in the twisted society he has returned to. As he gets the keys out, he thumbs through them, ever closer to the guard. The guard watches, and turns a touch to face Ben, folding his arms.

Ben pretends to find the key he's looking for and stops whistling. He takes the big bronze Yale house key in his right hand between thumb and forefinger, as if ready to open a door. He walks past the guard without even addressing him - and bursts into action with a sickening speed and ferocity.

He launches at the guard, leaping and coiling, and buries both knees into the guards chest, exploding him backward into the door he was supposed to be protecting. With his right hand, he drives the key into the guard's neck, and out again - it is an ugly blunt instrument for such a job, but the force of the hit drives the key into it's target fairly easily. Not a nice way to go. The guard crashes into the door and the sudden impact forces it to open. The guard falls backwards into the apartment, choking messily as he thuds onto the bare floorboards of the hall. The man writhes on the floor but only for a brief moment, as the skirting boards take a grim spattering of crimson spray from his neck.

Ben stands at the door and looks inside. Sunlight blazes and Manchester is presented in all it's glory through high floor to ceiling windows opposite the door. Freya sits with masking tape across her mouth on the floor by the window, and looks up at the commotion from the door. She appears to only be wearing a nighty. Even though she can't speak, her eyes tell all: how horrible what she just saw was, how relieved she is to see Ben and, on balance, given her desperate predicament, what an entrance that was.

5

The guard is barely on his back when Ben bends over him and opens his jacket, checking the inside breast pockets and under-arms for a firearm. The prone guard cackles softly, but Ben barely registers the horrors of the guard's last moments. He finds nothing - this may suggest that the man did not have a military background, but Ben can't be sure. Ex-military opposition would ramp up the difficulty of this situation considerably, and Ben hopes that this is a good sign.

He checks the guard's waistband, front and back. Nothing. He yanks up the guard's trouser-legs and checks. Still nothing. He knows he can't keep looking - the noise will have alerted Freya's kidnappers. Freya has been watching, and Ben looks up and catches her eye. His expression doesn't change a bit as he brings his finger up across his pursed mouth, gesturing a firm 'shhh'. She immediately looks down at the floor. Ben feels for her - in her nighty, on the floor, tear-speckled cheeks and the threat of oncoming demise. He has met Freya twice - she always seemed a nice girl. A safe bet for Trev - Trev's easy humour had always been attractive to the girls when he and Ben were in their teens. He had done well for himself, but he got the feeling Freya felt that she had done well in return. They were, in short, a nice deserving pair.

Hate swells in Ben, and he lets it roll out but not too far. He knows hate gives you an unbending steel when it comes to completing an unpleasant objective, but blind rage is exactly the opposite. He lowers himself to a crouch and peeks around the corner into the flat. First thing to strike Ben is that it's not very big - the open living room and kitchen space is perhaps only 200 square feet. There is a bedroom door off opposite the entrance hallway, and the kitchen is sparse, white modern and, oddly, free of people.

He breaks across to the kitchen, ducking as he goes, fully expecting the bedroom door to open at any time. It doesn't - he get's to the kitchen and dread begins to set in. Where is everybody? Are they all in the bedroom? What is happening? He reaches up to the kitchen draws to see what he can find. First one is just so chock-full of pans he can barely get it open. Second, is empty take-out boxes, about fifty of them. The third draw is a cutlery draw - bingo. He reaches his hand in - when the bedroom door blasts open. Ben's hand closes on whatever he can grasp, feels something metallic and pulls it out quickly. He crouches again, just as two men barrel into the room. He looks down at his hand - to see he is brandishing a soup spoon. Great, he thinks.

The two men are both crossing the room now, towards the entrance hallway. One of them is a squat powerhouse, a cube of human muscle. In this confined space, Ben knows he will be a nightmare to stop. A steroidal bull in a tiny China shop. It's a miracle that they could find a suit to fit him, let alone the sharp navy number he is wedged into. The other man is of average height but is so sprightly on his feet Ben almost misses him completely. He has crossed the room before Ben knows it. Two very different adversaries that, in the outside world, Ben would have no trouble taking on. But together, at the same time, in this tiny space, with Freya in the middle of it all? No way, he thinks - a different approach is needed.

By the way the men have trotted across the room, Ben has surmised that neither of these guys is the boss. On hearing Ben's entrance, the main man was never going to just poke his head around the door for Ben to have a crack at. He assumes the man must be in the bedroom. He leaps over the counter top, and motors straight for the bedroom door, opening it and flinging it shut behind him. He is not keen on leaving Freya alone, but considering their desire for the laptop, he is banking on them not touching her until they know where their prized possession is.

Inside the room a man in his sixties is quickly pulling his trousers up. The man turns to Ben, and his expression is indeed that of a man caught with his pants down. The expression turns to venom-fueled spite, as he clanks his belt clasp closed. He is tanned, grey, wrinkled, with sparkling blue daggers for eyes. Ben shudders at the thought of how many boys and girls have been seduced, betrayed and abused by those eyes over the years.

'Who the fuck are you?' the man spits. Ben answers with a forearm to the throat, hard and spiked, right into the man's adam's apple. The man bends, but doesn't crumple, and Ben holds him upright to face the door. Ben shifts right behind him and plunges his hand into the man's jacket pocket. He had noticed it as soon as he saw the man bending to pull his pants up - that heavy sag across the left breast-piece of the jacket. An unmistakable gun. As Ben's fingers touch it there is a horrid moment of reconnection within Ben's mind, as if he and the gun have a love-hate relationship borne out of experiences both good and bad, but predominantly awful - 'There you are, you bitch', 'Oh it's you again, couldn't stay away for long could you...'

Gun in hand he holds it to the man's head and thumbs off the safety. He pushes the man towards the door.

'Name' Ben states.

'Fuck off' the man offers, and Ben roughly pushes him towards the door and into the living room - where the other two men are now waiting. Steroid squat man holds Freya up by her hair, who writhes uncomfortably like a fish on the line. Ben can see dark bruises forming on her legs. The other man holds a gun against her chest. At the sight of their master with a gun to his head, they flinch slightly but maintain form.

Ben begins to speak slowly and clearly.

'You are to let her go or I end this man's life. Nothing can be gained from this situation anymore - the laptop is destroyed.'

This seems to stop everyone a little cold - apart from Freya, who still tries to stay upright despite being held out by her hair.

'If you want to take issue with anyone, it's me. The lady has no purpose or part of this anymore' Ben continues.

'Like hell she doesn't. She's our leverage now. You've done me quite the favour. Destroying the laptop destroys any evidence of our lovely little cash cow - I could thank you,' growls the man Ben holds. Ben pulls the man closer so his right ear is tight to Ben's mouth. He whispers.

'You are as low as anything I've come across. You are low-rent shit in a modest apartment. Nothing more. But I've got a big problem with you. You fucked with my friends. You are part of the plague this country finds itself swallowed in. I know exactly what you are: you are the vile central cog of an obscene child sex ring. You are as low as low gets - profiting from the gross sickness that is paedophilia. Your precious laptop is gone, and with it that empire. But I'm not sure. The only way to be sure, is to kill you and your friends here and now, and I'm here to wipe the dog shit off Manchester's heel.'

'Don't let her go, boys' says the man.

'Is that how you want to play this? You two - you want to play this too?' Ben asks.

'Fuck you. Kill her,' barks the man. Freya screams on hearing the words she has been dreading since the ordeal began.

'Finally, Keith,' replies steroid squat man.

Keith. The name resonates with Ben - every now and then, a name brings something to mind. Often it's to do with relationships or celebrity. For Ben, the name Keith will always be synonymous with evil.

Ben shoves Keith sharply into the kitchen, and drops to one knee. He calls to mind an occasion in Basra when he was hidden beneath a broken-down lorry on a roadside, and a member of his team had been captured by Taliban forces. As they were passing his position, he had to choose between letting them get away and probably execute his colleague, or shoot up their legs, knowing that that would not kill anyone, that the wounds would be severe, but if his colleague took a bullet or two, he would survive. That time, he fired his automatic weapon into the passing group of captors and captive. He managed to get his man out of there alive - just. His colleague took a bullet in the thigh (from Ben) and one in the shoulder (from the enemy). But he got him out of there. Now, Ben was holding a semi-automatic 9mm, a much more controlled weapon in an environment where there is only one other gun. The odds seemed pretty good to him.

Taking aim, Ben fired as carefully and as forcefully as he could at the group opposite him, while taking care to aim for trouser legs and not delicate female calves. The contrast in targets reminds him of his training and, somehow, 3 of the 6 shots fired hit trousers, with the other three hitting the wall behind. Poor tall guy, thinks Ben - didn't even get a shot away. It strikes Ben that they really weren't prepared for combat, or at least not the kind of highly trained combat and tactics that Ben would be bringing to proceedings. Ben ponders whether to show mercy and leave this scum to the authorities, then he remembers what was on the laptop. Mercy vanishes, and, as they hit the floor one at a time, bullet holes in their lower legs, he finishes them both off with the remaining two slugs in the clip. Freya is left standing over the two men, and again, shock permeates her features.

Ben's eyes dart left, as Keith sprints for the door. Ben is firmly in command now, and he starts to sprint after him, and as he passes Freya, he grabs her hand. They run out of the apartment, hopping over the body of the key-slashed doorman, and down the corridor after Keith. Keith is running for his life, ragged and panicked - but his age slows him.

'Take this right - opposite 3267 is a secret door in the wood panelling. Look for the keyhole. Trev is beyond it. Go with him - NOW' Ben lets go of Freya, who slows to look at him.

'Thank you' she says with feeling.

'GO.' Ben says firmly.

Freya starts to continue running. People are emerging into the hallway, having heard the commotion. Ben wants to make sure she gets out but doesn't really want to risk someone getting a great ID of him or losing Keith. He presses on, and, for Freya and Trev, hopes for the best.

After ten more strides, he is almost on Keith. It hits Ben how pathetic an adversary Keith is, but how awful his crimes are. The minute you turn your back in a town like this, it seems a vile puke with some awful ideas will regurgitate horrors on the unsuspecting. Keith will get everything he deserves.

Keith is running out of both breath and corridor - up ahead is a huge window. He slows to a canter, the window and the horizon beyond becoming a haunting reminder of the freedom he had only moments ago - before this vigilante do-gooder decided to concern himself with his dealings. He turns and walks the last couple of paces to the window backwards, so he can face Ben.

Ben has no bullets left in the gun, but knows he won't need it. He knows Keith doesn't have another, and Keith's body-language betrays a submission that he is very unfamiliar with. Ben thinks of all the poor girls, of all ages, Keith has towered over. He stops himself, before the hate gets too much, ten feet from Keith, and checks behind him. A couple of faces peep around ajar front doors, too scared to come out fully, which is a relief to Ben.

He thinks about saying something to Keith - one last sign off, but he holds himself. He has said everything he needs to - Keith will go to Hell knowing it. He picks up a short, two stride sprint, and leaps into the air in a dropkick - two feet forward. At the point of impact, he kicks out both legs fully, kicking and stretching with as much brute power he can muster. One foot connects with Keith's chest, the other with the point of his nose. The effect is devastating to Keith. Ben picked these points of impact for two reasons. Firstly, the pain of his boot shattering Keith's nose will cause Keith's body to stiffen rigid as a board. Secondly, the boot in the chest will shove the board-like body at high speed into the glass. Ben reasoned the combined effect would be just enough to fracture the enforced safety glass of the window - and it does just that, with a vile, wet crack. Ben hears the soft whisper of wind, as Keith's body crumples.

Ben knows the main problem with breaking the window was always going to be that first crack, but that's no longer a problem. As Keith slumps, his nose at a disastrous and unfixable angle, Ben catches him.

'The pain you've caused will never leave those girls, but all that pain you might cause in future is going with you to the pavement below.'

Keith gags angrily as if to tell Ben where to get off, but his busted nose and the blood flowing from it into his mouth won't let him. Even to his last moment he is a gross depiction of defiance who fails to recognize a shred of evil in what he has done - which makes Ben's next action all the easier. He swings Keith, with one hand on his lapel and one on his waistband, straight at the centre of the window. The glass gives with no resistance. The safety shield of the glass holds firm at the window edges, so the glass simply parts on the crack to allow Keith through, like a huge, jagged, transparent door. Keith slides through the widening crack, buffeted by the force, and suddenly, he is outside, howling and going down very fast. Gone.

Ben takes the tablespoon from his pocket, and throws it out after him, down to the waking street below. He waits to hear an impact, but none arrives. His eyes drift to the vista of the city, thinking of all the other hidden horrors this society might have to offer.

With the threat neutralised, his hangover comes back almost immediately, as if someone hoovered his adrenaline away to reveal his true ugly state beneath. No time yet for wallowing. He needs to get out - he doesn't give a a damn about the police knowing it was him, but he doesn't want them to find out when he's in their custody. That would be no good at all. He picks up another explosive sprint, and heads back down the corridor, and takes the left turn back for the hidden door he sent Freya to. He hopes, above all else, that they made it - he has a feeling that they did, and he clings to it with resolve.

6

Trev has gone through the whole range of emotions today, and he feels it. His brain aches from what he has seen and felt - the horrors of watching Ben maim those women, the lows of losing Freya and the threat of her death, and the sheer spiraling high of having her back.

But he knows that precisely none of it compares to what Freya has been through. He looks at her, sitting next to him on the sofa back in their Northern Quarter apartment. The place is still pretty much destroyed, but they are safe and together. He pulls her close. She is holding a coffee. Trev didn't have one - he's still trying to lose the taste of the super coffee he hastily poured down his gullet earlier.

'Do you think he got out?' asks Freya, her knees bunching up under her.

'Yes, I do' Trev replies. Trev didn't know if he was lying or not.

'We'll have to invite him over at Christmas' says Freya. Trev smiles.

'Yes we will' he says. Out of the stillness, his phone beeps. He checks it, shifting Freya gently so he can reach into his pocket. It's a text message from Ben.

'YOU WON'T SEE ME FOR A WHILE. AFTER READING THIS, DELETE MY CONTACT DETAILS IN THE PHONE. GO TO THE POLICE. TELL THEM WHAT HAPPENED - GET THE HELP YOU NEED. REGARDING WHAT HAPPENED UP THERE, TELL THEM EVERYTHING. I HAVE A NAME TO CLEAR'

Trev reads the message twice. And smiles grimly. He shows Freya, who silently reads it and digests it. God knows what Ben did up there, but Trev knows it was in the name of good. He flicks through his contacts, and brings up Ben's name, to which he clicks another button. The phone asks him:

DELETE CONTACT: BEN BRACKEN?

Trev pauses, then slowly presses the green affirmative command. And with that Ben Bracken was gone - his whereabouts unknown.

THE BARONESS

1

Something wakes Michael up. Not sharply, merely that soft tug of reality you experience when in the warm squeeze of a deep sleep. Consciousness won't release it's grip, as he tries to ignore it and slip back into the dark tranquility he was so happy in seconds before. His eyes crack open, and he knows that that's it - he's up.

Damn it, he thinks. He has a long overnight shift coming up, and he really can't afford to be missing his rest - as the overnight security guard at Llechwedd Slate Caverns, it is hard enough at times in that inky abyss down there, without the threat of drowsiness. As he sits vaguely annoyed, his frustration is gradually overtaken by another nagging feeling - that something is not right.

He rolls over - the bed is empty, but that is exactly what he expected. Sharon hasn't spent the night with him in far too long - he still loves her, but he barely ever sees her. She is away with her new man, that smarmy piece of gutter slime in Bangor, about 20 minutes away by car. For all intents and purposes, he is single now and he must get used to it. However hard that may be.

The room is dark, the curtains tight shut, but the soft light of dusk beyond permeates the fabric. His senses sharpen one at a time, search each other out and bond - he is coming round. And it's as he comes round he realizes what woke him - a soft, high-pitched whistling. He is up straight away, tugging on the dirty jeans by his bed and hopping/buttoning them as he gets to the bedroom door.

When out into the hallway, the whistling is a touch louder but not by much. He marches down the hall, which doesn't take long in his old bungalow - an old miner's cottage on the edge of Llanberis, Snowdonia, North Wales. It is usually warm, with the faded carpets getting sparser every year, but somehow retaining a quaint cosiness. This evening, however, it is a little cold inside, which peaks Michaels concern a touch higher.

He knows he could shout for Sharon, but that would be too much like wishful thinking. It would be purely wasted energy, but Sharon isn't his primary concern - his thoughts are with Matthew, his 3 month old son. Matthew's room is back up the corridor next to the master bedroom, but he is such a light sleeper that Michael was hesitant firstly, to shout, and secondly, to disturb his boy. He knows if he disturbs him, his grandmother, Michael's mother, will pay for it through the night. Sharon had decided within moments of Matthew's birth, that she was unready for motherhood - and the effect on all of them had been both dramatic and traumatic. Michael's job couldn't bend to meet the burden of being a single father, so their routine had to accommodate his hours. He is relieved his son is such a good sleeper.

As Michael walks back down the corridor from whence he came, he notices the whistling again - and it's increase in volume. And as he gets closer to Matthew's door, it is clear that the whistling is beyond it. He pauses by the door and listens. Yes, he thinks, definitely whistling. He thinks for a second that it must be the baby monitor, that is running out of batteries, or going faulty for whatever reason. He holds his breath and creaks the door open.

As he opens the nursery door, and pokes his head around, he sees the familiar modest kids' room - animal prints on the walls, stuffed animals on the floor, clothes folded loosely on the changing unit, the vast cot. The only thing that's missing from the setting is the child itself - the cot is empty. Michael is struck by a wave of sick dizziness, the kind that only a parent will ever know when fear for their offspring kicks in. This dizziness becomes a full-on feverish panic when he sees the window open by an inch or two, the soft twilight breeze rattling against the old window frame, causing that eerie, haunting whistle as it enters the room.

Michael almost can't even speak, his words clogging in his throat as panic for his boy surges. He searches the room desperately. He can't really crawl, he can't have gone far, thinks Michael, desperately. But he knows the worst has happened. Every parents nightmare. Unless Matthew stood up and reached out of his cot to open the window, then somehow climbed out, which seems desperately fantastical, his only son has been snatched.

Moments later, Michael is sprinting as fast as his jellied legs can carry him, into Llanberis - a quiet village which is part tourist-trap, part hikers'-retreat on the banks of Padarn Lake. Michael is mid-thirties, and not in the best shape, so as he rounds the road into the high street, he cuts a rather pudgy, wheezing figure. He knows where he is going though - in the quiet autumn months, when the tourists have all gone back to whence they came, the locals occupy the only pub that's not an over-priced, faux-trendy, gastro-pub, love-in. And he can see it on the horizon. The Flapper and Firkin. A stone pub embodying every tradition that the pub trade seems to have forgotten in recent years - a warm welcome, with a tasty, locally-sourced pint. Perfection ordinarily, and on his nights off, Michael can often be seen in there shooting the breeze with whoever might be supping. Plus, with it being firmly a local haunt, the secrets of the village are laid bare within those four walls on a nightly basis - and if anyone knows anything, that would be the place to start.

As soon as he had caught his breath back at the cottage, he had called the police. Hopelessly, they had said, that if the mother is missing also, doesn't that suggest that the child is out with her? Michael had no answer for that, only to argue blindly that Sharon is no longer active in the family home, let alone in the role of mother, and that the window was uncharacteristically open. The thought had occurred to him that Sharon might indeed have the boy, but, while selfish, she isn't stupid. She wouldn't dream of taking the boy without Michael knowing.

With a gasp, he starts ascending the stone steps of the pub, and slings the doors open. He is greeted by a dark mahogany-clad interior and five or six men, who slowly turn to face the exhausted arrival.

'My son is gone!' shouts Michael. 'Someone snatched him from his cot!'

All the other men fall silent and look at each other, in shock at Michael's words - except for one. A stranger at the bar, who Michael doesn't recognize. He is younger than the others, but wears the same concern. He is wearing an old red shirt, black pants and a dark coat. He stands up from his barstool immediately.

The man walks over to Michael quickly, looking tired and down-trodden, but moving with a strength and alertness. His blue eyes fix on Michael and the urgency in them pins him to the spot.

'Where was he last seen?' asks Ben Bracken.

2

Ben was on the cusp of a deep reverie when the man burst in. He had just bought his fourth pint of Blackstoke Bitter, and was enjoying the familiar musty comfort blanket that only the fourth pint can bring. He has been in Wales for three weeks, keeping his head down and going about a quiet, self-indulgent wallow in seemingly the middle of nowhere. From the events of the last couple of minutes, Ben thought, the middle of nowhere sure has its own problems. And this one is a real nasty one.

The mention of a child missing is an emotive one to Ben, for many reasons. So many times during his forced tenure behind enemy lines, he had witnessed first-hand catastrophic cruelty towards children - really young children too. The effect of this on him had always left him light-headed. In darker moments, he clung to this dizziness -it meant that fundamentally he was a good man with a solid moral fibre that was undoubtedly there, no matter how far down he was sometimes forced to bury it.

Seeing this man panic in that oh-so-familiar way, snapped Ben back to his time in Afghanistan, to an environment and time that prevented him from acting.

There was damn well nothing stopping him now. If there was anything he could do to save this child tonight, he would do it. He would not make that same mistake again, and hope to whatever powers that be, that this would somehow make up for all the times behind enemy lines when he was handcuffed to inaction. For Ben, fixing time looms, and he will make every last pressing second count.

Ben recognizes the man in the loosest sense, in that they've been in the pub at approximately the same time more than once in the last three weeks. He approaches him with purpose.

'When did you last see him?' he asks with authority. The sternness and no-nonsense delivery of his words command a straight answer, which Michael, unsure and confused, is forced to give.

'About 2pm, at home, in his crib,' Michael offers.

'And the child's mother?'

'I don't know. She has a new man in Bangor.'

'Where is your home?'

'Around the side of the lake.'

'At the bottom of the hill below the mountain hospital?'

'That's right.' Ben was pleased to hear this. He was familiar with the area.

'Who knows where the child was?'

'No one, as far as I know. Who are you?'

'Call me Ben. I'll head for the hillside.' Ben looks at him, and watches momentarily how he is gulping for air. 'You are to go home and call the police again. Tell them everything.'

'I'm coming with you. We are talking about my son! He needs his father!' Michael bursts, the panic rising. His desire to be close to his child has never been so fierce and bubbling.

'Your son may need quick decisive action without compromise or question. Given the physical exertion and panic you are experiencing I don't think you are best placed to offer this. You are going home, and you are to wait there.'

That tone of authority, with its unwavering spine of firm instruction, simultaneously settles Michael into the idea and lets him know that this really is the best option. There is milage in the idea of going home and manning the land line - Christ knows the encroaching mountains generally put paid to the notion of any consistent phone reception.

'Why the hillside?' Michael asks.

'A hunch' Ben responds, and heads for the door. 'Besides - you snatch a child, you are hardly going to parade through town with him. The hill is the quietest way out of the valley. I'll do everything I can, and I won't stop till we get him back. You have my word.'

And with that, Ben thrusts open the door and stomps out into the night. Before the door can even swing shut on the gawping faces inside the pub, Ben's footsteps have increased in frequency, and decreased in audibility - wherever he is going, he is sprinting as if his life depends on it.

3

As Ben pounds the tarmac around the lake, he really gets a sense of the natural beauty the area has to offer. Rolling hills peppered by dramatic firs, over a glassy expanse of pure lakeside. If it wasn't for the obviously horrible set of circumstances, it is dusky Welsh-land at its absolute finest. There is a church high on the hill over the glassy mirror of Padarn below, set in deep tree-line. Ben knows roughly where, thanks to what can only be described as his incessant armed forces urges. He can't help it. So many occasions he'd been caught with his cartographical pants down because he had been supplied poor intel, or, in the earlier days, hadn't done his own homework. First morning he arrived, he scoped the whole area out.

When he had first seen the dilapidated church, he had thought it might be the perfect place to set up in if the police came for him, or if he got himself into any scrapes. He wasn't in any unexpected conflicts yet, but that adrenaline surge hitting his muscles like a hot acid bath usually meant one thing - something is coming. He knows the church is only about 500 yards up the hillside, above the old mountain hospital - which itself, is now shut and merely functions as a tourist hotspot. The light is failing, but he knows his intel is good. He'd make it within the next few moments.

Ben loves Wales on a deep yet unfathomable level. He has been here many many times in his infancy, with his doting, long-dead grandparents. They always loved him no matter what - much more so than his parents, who, despite his return from the darkest places the earth has to offer, want nothing in the slightest to do with him. All they could see was the dishonourable discharge stamp - and nothing else. The sacrifices he had made were completely lost on them, and they were more worried about the impact on the Bracken family name than anything else. He often wonders whether his grandparents would have followed suit, or whether they would be more forgiving like way back when he was just a kid. He clings to the latter stubbornly.

As he sprints around the lake, he remembers Manchester, and what had happened. He knows the police are after him, but he gets the idea that they hadn't looked as hard as they might have... Who knows, thinks Ben - they may be just around the corner with a wagon full of tactical support. All Ben knows is that he is outside of the law, even though his heart, body and soul is committed to the protection of it. To what extent he would be prepared to go to always ends up blurring that line...

It was different for him though. He had been in combat, and had been in the most high-octane pressure-jacked environments, when the very foundations of who you are become exposed and frayed like naked wires in a sandstorm. And as he spies the church on the crest of the brow above, framed by branches of fir against an ever-deepening azure canvas, the scene looks anything but traumatic. If anything, it looks a bit too normal - like when you visit the real-life location of a horror film, only to realize that when it is stripped of atmosphere and artistic framing, there's nothing scary about the place at all. But, Ben thinks, bring Wes Craven up here, and this place would be an iconic a horror venue as any.

The church is a single story stone effort, with a small spire. It could adorn any village green anywhere in rural Britain - the only difference here being that it is largely boarded up, with odd bits of garbage and old furniture outside. Yet, beyond, somewhere inside, there is unmistakable hint of life. There are no cars outside, but Ben knows that the place is not empty. That instinct is only confirmed by the flickering light poking through the hastily hung boards over the windows. To Ben, that inches the horror feel even further, and he is not glad for it - horror movies were never his bag. Ever. He's always been calm when faced with a human, factual adversary - something he can see and feel - but the prospect of something different, something unknown, scares him. And when faced with something like now, that is in reality, yet somehow carries a whisper of the unknown... it freaks him out. He imagines pulling focus in his mind, like looking through a lens and twisting focal point to find the truth. Get past the muddled surroundings and zoom into the real deal and bring it into sharpness. And today the real deal is a missing child. The thought bursts a prickling clarity through every corner of Ben's brain.

As he approaches the church, he slows to more of a crouched walk and finds the nearest corner of the front wall. Silence still pervades, and he pauses to a standstill to listen. He can't hear a damn thing. Well, the birds around the church are all singing goodnight to each other, but something that gives away a sign of human life? Nothing.

Ben sneaks along, to the nearest window, and tries to peek through the boards. They are too tightly arranged for him to see through, but higher up, there are a few cracks between the slats which were obviously harder for the joiner to nail in straight. Down in front of the window, on the floor, is an upturned wooden table, like an extremely basic, carved, spindly turtle. One of it's legs is missing, prompting Ben to grab one of the other ones and rip it off like a chicken leg - and now he has a weapon, albeit an extremely primitive one.

He scolds himself. Has he been too hasty? Is he letting his emotions and the creepiness of the setting get to him? What happens if there's a knitting meeting going on in there? What if he is wasting time here, while the child-snatcher is making off into the night with the poor lad? Yeah right, he thinks - what maniacs come up to an abandoned church at dusk for a little evening out? He edges past the table, and further long the wall, getting ever closer to the front door. The door is large, wooden and looks so old that a fierce yank might pull it straight off it's hinges. Ben attempts to test that theory, and throwing caution to the wind, pulls the rusted handle as hard as he can.

To his surprise, the door offers no resistance at all. In fact, it opens far too easily, suggesting that not only is it still actively used but someone may have actually applied oil to the hinges to keep them in good shape. Creepsville has a janitor, he thinks, as warm light seeps from inside the church and splashes onto his face like Holy Water itself. His eyes take a second to adjust, but as they do, he is shocked to see he can make out a warm, well-kept church with, even more shockingly, a full congregation in there. Each pew has a few people on it, who all appear over 50 or so. And they are silent. Horribly silent. There must be 40 or so of them, and they crane around to peer at him. They all look so relaxed, sedate and quiet. Ben is confused, and can't for the life of him fathom what they might be doing. It must be bad, he reasons. If not, why do it in an abandoned church at nightfall, he thinks.

Survival instinct kicks in, and he realizes he needs an upper hand. Stealth hasn't worked, and his cover is well blown. If he plays to that instinct, the upper hand is theirs, so he feels he must act like the whole thing is planned. With that, he hoists the table leg up to rest on his shoulder, and puts a hand on his hip.

'Well, what in the good name of fuck is going on here, then?' he bellows. His voice echoes around the hall, and it's belligerence shocks him - he knew he was going to apply a modicum of bravado, but did he really have to crank it all the way up to cocksure lager lout?

The people remain still and calm. This unnerves Ben more than most things he's ever experienced, but since he's gone all-in, he presses on with a stride down the aisle.

'If I didn't know better, I'd say there was something extremely fishy going on around here' he taunts, his eyes casting around the room. Exits front and back, windows low enough to dive through if he managed to take a leap off a pew. Pew's are pretty full, though.

He paces down the aisle, and comes to a stop. He keeps uncharacteristically fighting off the odd wave of panic as he walks - he has seen something like this once or twice before, when he was in captivity deep behind enemy lines. The Taliban prayers had been insistent and intoxicating, and had utterly consumed the men holding him and pressed them down into this mellowed state. What he learnt from that experience was that, despite how serene the exterior, below boils a fanaticism that is only matched by it's unwavering commitment. He had been scared then, and he's scared now. Doesn't matter how old you are, approximately 40 to 1 is bad odds any hour. He turns as he reaches the altar, and faces the congregation - a mad, table-leg wielding preacher with his silent creepy flock.

Suddenly another voice breaks the stillness, strong, resonating and female, like the voice you'd perhaps imagine belonging to Big Sister.

'What are your intentions, outsider?' she bellows.

4

There is often in life a moment that defines you - separates all the various components, shines them up bright and clear, then fuses them together in a composite whole. After the epiphany, you are somehow better than before - version 2.0. As Ben whisks around to face the owner of the voice, he can't help feeling that this could well be one of those moments.

By the time he has spun 180, and has tried to focus, he realizes he can't see the source. The voice is still, echoing, a booming vocal blast bouncing off every wall of the church - dominating and oddly painful. As he was rotating, the stained glass windows had created a lurid, blurred zoetrope, that, strangely now he is stationary, is now etched on his retinas like rainbow vomit. And for some reason, his eyes can not see past the colored blobs and whirls. He shakes his head, but just can't rearrange the color into something meaningful. The voice is still booming, but he can't make out the words. He drops slowly to one knee, to try to regain some composure and his table leg clunks on the floor.

Ben strains and takes a few deep breaths - long in and long out. Whenever he does this, he can almost feel the oxygen flood the recesses of his brain, and for a mere second, his vision comes back briefly - and he sees a snapshot of a statuesque light-haired woman standing by the altar in a red dress. As soon as his sight has had time to give him something to work with, the edges smudge, the borders blur, and he's back to wading through a visual miasma.

Something else has presented itself, which Ben sensed when he saw the woman. The incense ain't incense. While he had that moment of clarity, he noticed that it was copal. While he was training for the armed forces, he had done some extremely remote time in Central America, learning survival techniques in jungle settings and that's where he had come across it. Copal was frequently used by some indigenous societies in sweat lodge ceremonies - to aid in purification, and the driving out of demons. What the hell it is doing in North Wales is utterly beyond Ben, but there is something else nasty at play, and it has given itself away with a dark, bitter after-taste to the scent. LSD. Surprisingly, there is also a smaller sweetness on the furthermost tip of his tongue. Marijuana. As Ben's tries to keep all his facets together, he can't help his thoughts clouding darkly just as bad as his vision. Just what the fuck is going on here?

Before he has finished his thought, he feels an awful sharp thud on the back of his head, as if he has been hit with something - he can't tell what, but he can sure feel it. Warm begins to pour down the side of his head, onto his cheek, and he binds his eyes shut to beat back the pain and keep from getting what can only be his own blood in his eyes. The dizziness doubles.

The voice ramps up in intensity, and he can make out the occasional word -

'........purge.........hate...........worth...........pound.....
....outsider ('that old chestnut', Ben thinks).........fear.........price........'

Ben didn't like any of those words, frankly. He still has no idea what is going on, but it is becoming increasingly apparent that if there is a young baby around these nutjobs, burning drugs and talking about a 'purge', that can only be a bad thing. If the child is up here, Ben knows he has to get it together. He's not up on this dank hillside on a jolly.

Abruptly, Ben sticks his fingers down his throat, triggering his gag reflex. Almost immediately, he throws up - a lot. Blackstoke Bitter drenches the steps at the bottom of the altar, splattering wetly against the stone of the church floor. For Ben, the taste is awful, but he has to get all that vile airborne concoction out of his body as quickly as he can, before he loses control altogether.

The abrupt retching had cut short the woman's ranting, but the woman's voice punctuates the gagging once more, but this time bearing a venomous call to arms.

'Punish this man. Punish him for questioning. Punish him for jeopardizing the purge! He does not want you to reach God - are you going to let him stop you from serving the Almighty?!'

Ben is both pleased and not pleased. Pleased that he heard every word and his drug-blurred mindset allowed him to arrange the words correctly. However, he is most definitely not pleased at the prospect of being torn limb from limb by some angry senior citizens. From his crouch, he spreads his arms around the floor, trying to find something through his hazy vision with which he can defend himself. His hands rake through his own vomit.

'Oh, for Christ's sake...' he mutters, moving his hands through - then his outstretched fingers bump something solid. He averts his eyes to the object and can just make out that he is touching his table leg - and has never felt so relieved to see a piece of busted home furniture. He curls his fingers around it tight.

Suddenly, a cold firm hand grasps around his ankle. Ben hadn't even realized the flock were up and moving. Without hesitation, from it's resting position on the floor, he swings the table leg at full force, calculating the trajectory as the leg is in flight with a little monologue to himself: 'If the hand is on my ankle, the assailant is in a crouch or bending, therefore, taking into account the average height of over 65's at 5 feet 7 inches, the optimum height to swing the club for impact above my foot is about there -' CRACK. Another happy customer.

Ben's vision is coming back quickly now, but he knows he has to find the source of the incense before that horrible haze comes straight back. He looks to where he made contact with his makeshift bat, and there is a bald man lying slumped on the floor with a huge gash atop his fleshy wrinkled skull. Ben doesn't take any pride in maiming the old fellow, but God knows what the High Priestess of this awful congregation is able to make them do. And Ben knows, for every weird and awful thing that happens here, the likelihood of the child being safe and staying that way gets further and further distant.

He stands, and, as he surveys what awaits him, the scene begins to resemble some kind of zombie apocalypse. Swathes of people who approaching him menacingly - not with that lumbering gait of the undead from the Romero movies, more with a clear-eyed, single-mindedness fettered by the capabilities of the older demographics body type. They approach him with a purpose that, on making eye contact, is very real. And then he spots her - the High Priestess, the Baroness, running down the aisle to the front of the church, her arms bunched and folded tightly below her chest. Ben knows that, unless she is somehow injured, that's got to be the baby.

Ben thinks at this point that, if he was a religious man, he should really ask for some sort of forgiveness - here in God's house, he's going to have to dish out some nasty punishment to these people, men and women, in order to save the supposed infant. He thinks that these people should be the one's begging for forgiveness, not him. Truth is, from a theological standpoint, Ben doesn't know what he believes. He has seen enough horrors whose very existence warrants the belief that no God could exist, but then again, nobody guaranteed that God would be ambivalent. Either way, cracking a few OAP skulls in a church doesn't sit right with Ben, and he reaches into the furthest nooks of his mind for some words for forgiveness, perhaps something he can remember from school. All he can think of is the Lord's prayer, and a pre-dinner prayer for Grace. Since he has no intention of dying here, he opts for the latter, albeit modified.

'Umm... For what we are about to receive, may the Lord make me truly... sorry' he says. He knows he botched it, but at least he tried. That must count for at least something if he pops it and finds himself pitched up unexpectedly at the pearly gates. And with that he starts running and swinging at the oncoming horde.

To the casual outsider, the scene would most definitely cut a disconcerting sight - a half-cut bloke swinging a table leg at a pastel-clad army of senior citizens. It would certainly go a long way to increasing the amount of jail time he might face if he is ever forced to face justice. SMACK goes the wood into an older lady's shoulder, then THUNK straight into an older man's chest. It feels awful to Ben, just the most unnatural thing to do ever. He was always raised to respect his elders, not bring them an ugly battering. What he is doing turns his stomach, but he knows it is not the first time he has had to do something truly abhorrent in order to survive.

He swings again, with no target in mind, simply to make debilitating contact and swing again - only this time the wood, on making contact, almost sticks to it's victim like it was bogged in tar. Ben tries to pull it out and back to him, but the wood is tugged away from him. He feels his finger loosening on the wood, and then some more fingers clawing through his hairline. An old lady is literally trying to scalp him with her own withered hands. Ben can only think 'This is definitely a first'. A punch hits him right in the breadbasket, which is a devastating impact, so penetrating, that Ben is pretty sure the owner of the fist will have grazed his knuckles on Ben's own vertebrae, right through his stomach. It hurts Ben a lot. One of these boys has got some real power, Ben thinks. Through sheer force of will he refuses to go down, driven by the fear that the moment he does go down, he's pretty sure he won't get up again.

He pulls his head up again, to take in some air, where he can see his own weapon of terror swinging down onto the top of his skull - no longer has he managed to get upright, and the table leg has been used to smash him right in the head. The impact is too much this time. Ben slumps, and all he can see is blood vessels in his vision - tiny swirling blobs that the mere sight of can't be anything good. That odd cold glove of unconsciousness begins to entrench Ben, and he almost welcomes it. He falls, hands clawing at his clothes, dragging him this way and that.

Suddenly, a deafening blast rips through the church. It silences the hordes and punishes the ear drums. Ben is suddenly dropped onto his front on the church floor, as his oppressors fan. He has no idea where the sound came from, but he knows it stopped his torment, and for that, he is grateful. He can now see a black vignette at the corners of his vision, giving the sensation of seeing life through an Instagram filter - so an appropriate level of hipster drama is afforded what he sees happen next. An old man in a green waterproof jacket, paces down the aisle towards Ben, and he is wielding a mean-looking smoking shotgun.

'Get away from him!' he orders. 'Back! Back!'.

The man is cradling the shotgun tightly, but jabs it in the direction of the people he passes. He is older, like the people in the church, but, unlike the people in the church, there is a fire and fear in his eyes - as well as an absurd red blotchiness to his skin. The man keeps moving at a steady pace, then his boots are by Ben's nose.

'Can you stand?' he asks.

'Yes,' Ben answers, trying to hoist himself up to his knees, but manages only to lose his balance and roll onto his back like a stricken turtle.

'Can you bollocks,' the man scowls. Before Ben can try to get an idea of who the man might be, he can feel himself being hoisted to his feet. 'Get your bearings. Lean on me, but we need to move now.'

And with that, Ben is practically being dragged down the aisle back towards the front door.

'Any of you dare move, I'll bloody drop you', barks the man at the people, who just stare back glass-eyed like the sheep that they are. 'Nearly there,' he whispers to Ben.

'Who are you?' croaks Ben.

'You've no idea?' the man replies.

Ben remains silent.

'"That'll be £2.90", does that ring a bell?'

'The pub' Ben replies.

'Yes, the pub. You've been my best customer for the last three weeks.'

Ben looks up to him and scrutinizes him - he can't, for the life of him, recognize him.

'Don't strain yourself', says the man. 'You never look up from up your pint. Ever. My name is Dag.'

5

Before Ben can look where they are going, they are outside. The cold air hits him immediately, like iced smelling salts, and invigorates him to the core. He chugs on the chilled oxygen, finally able to get his lungs to some clean, untainted air. It is most welcome, as is the effect it brings. Clarity begins to return. Dag keeps speaking, but let's Ben go - aware that his strength and wherewithal are returning.

'I literally shouted to you as you were heading out the door, back at the pub' Dag continues, as he looks for something with which to bolster the church door shut, to keep the weirdos contained. 'I wanted to come with you, as I had the shotgun. Bet you wish you'd waited.'

'I didn't hear,' Ben responds between breaths.

'You were gone before I'd even got my words up. Look, I can spot ex-military a mile off.'

Ben looks up with that honed defensiveness, prickly to whenever the military is mentioned - all too aware of it's divisiveness in the public sphere.

'You needn't worry, son, we know our own. The Welsh Guards, 1963.'

'The Rifles, 2013.' Ben responds. He wants to spill the rest but he knows he should not.

'Well, Rifles - there is a bonfire kicking off on the hill behind the Church, another couple of hundred yards up. I'll keep this ghost army at bay, while you go up there.'

'Thank you, Dag.' Ben offers earnestly.

Dag drags an old couch across the front door, then turns to Ben. 'I can't speak for anyone in there. I recognize a lot of those old boys. Down in the village we knew something was going on up here, but didn't know what. It was getting quieter at nights down there, but that's it. We always left them to it up here. But this... this... doesn't look good.'

'I have a thing for dropping in on bad situations' says Ben. 'You kind of get the feeling for them after a while, but this one is a little out there for me. Am I losing my mind, or does it appear that that old lady who ran out of here is preparing some kind of child sacrifice in a pseudo-voodoo mold?'

'I think I would find it very hard to argue against that,' Dag responds.

'Call the police - get them up here as fast as you can. If all goes well, you won't see me again. If it doesn't... Either way, thank you for helping me back there. I'm Ben Bracken. Make sure the police know that.'

'I can do that' Dag agrees, even though he has got no idea why this guy would want the police to know anything.

Ben turns to go, but Dag speaks again.

'The old adage is that "the army can change a man". They never tell you in what way - it's different for every man. Let whatever happened go, and move forward. Not everyone can say they have much of a life after the army - you have an opportunity to do good.'

Ben considers this. 'Believe it or not, that's exactly what I'm about to do. Sort of.'

Ben starts to run for the hill, while, behind him, Dag sighs and takes aim at the door. He knows he can fend them off, but he needs to keep them away from Ben and the bonfire as long as possible - for Dag, it feels like a chance to save the town. For all that is good and Holy, it is a chance he must take.

Ben glances upwards, at the ever-darkening sky. He navigates the terrain easily, his eyes growing more and more accustomed to the low light conditions. High overhead, he can see black smoke darkly clouding the tips of the trees, and his heart sinks - the fire is certainly burning up here, just like Dag said. He can't quite believe it, as the facts begin to mount. Aside from a family Guy Fawkes night, he can't think of any other occasion at all that would call for a baby to be present at a lit night-time bonfire. He didn't want to believe it was voodoo at all, but all the evidence points to it. The church, the baroness, the oppressed congregation, the violence, the phraseology, the fucking copal, the baby... Jesus, thinks Ben - I came here as a kid. I came here to find refuge, and I find as dark a fleapit of human debasement as I could hope to find. An innocent child. An innocent child!

Without thinking, Ben is moving faster, and soon, he can see the tips of the flames dancing up at the stars, and he knows he is close. One more slight rise. His knees ache and throb, and his lungs fizz with each intake of breath. Mercifully, the oxygen intake has almost completed it's job of clearing his mind and thoughts, and he knows that if he can keep his rage in check, he can bring a cool air of tactics to what may happen next. But then he remembers he has absolutely no training for saving a baby from a quasi-voodoo sacrifice - he'll follow his instincts, and his gut.

He slows at the peak, and slowly peeps his head over the crest, and he puts together a quick assessment of the scene, as if he is about to report his findings back to a superior officer. A clearing approximately 10 metres by 10 metres. A fairly large fire just back left of centre. Three rows of low wood benches facing the bonfire. A small stone altar in front of the fire, with a swaddled object atop it. The noisy crackle of the bonfire, and above that, punctuated and soft... an infant cry. It hits Ben hard - it's the first time he has had concrete evidence the child is even here. He feels both horrified and vindicated.

The woman appears from behind the bonfire, carrying what looks like a white plastic supermarket bag. Ben knows that despite how he'd like to assess the scene further, he may never get a chance to separate the woman and the infant, so he makes his presence felt.

'Stop there, you psychotic old bitch', he barks, as he runs into the clearing. He knows that if he gets close enough, his physical presence will root the woman to the spot. He'll have to judge where to stop, because too close and she will surely panic and go for the child. Too far back and he won't have any chance to reach the child even if he tried. He picks a spot and sticks to it.

'You have done enough harm to this community. This is where it stops,' Ben commands. The woman looks at him with curiosity and it's the first time Ben has had the chance to really look at her. She is tall, no doubt, and, on this further inspection, could be anywhere in age between 50 and 65. She has a shock of peroxide blond hair, cut in a cruel and uncompromising bob. She wears a red blazer with a cross pinned to the right lapel, over a tartan skirt. Facially, she passes more than a slight resemblance to Meryl Streep, but Ben feels that could just be the copal talking. She is ten feet from the altar, but Ben would like that to be more.

'I'm 15 feet from you. I can get to you and put you on your back within two and a half seconds. Get on your knees now, so that I don't have to do that,' Ben orders.

The woman smiles - a vile, smug, pursed grin. Ben dearly would love to wipe it off her face with his boot, if it didn't make him feel so unnerved. She speaks.

'Who are you to say what should or should not happen to the child?' she spits.

'I put that same question right back to you,' Ben retorts.

'If you knew what I know about this child, about what is demanded, you would be assisting me, not apprehending me.'

'At no point, ever, is the sacrifice of an infant acceptable or justified.'

'And you're evidence for this is...?', the Baroness asks. Ben wants to answer about moral fibre and code, and simple right and wrong, but he knows none of that applies now. The simmering, acidic determination in the woman's eyes confirm that they are long past negotiation. 'You have no knowledge of the darkness that surrounds us, that surrounds this place, that surrounds the child.'

'I know darkness. I've lived darkness. I'll show you darkness, if you like.' Ben retorts grimly. He coils his body, ready to pounce. But, with unexpected speed, the woman reaches into the carrier bag and pulls out a curved knife with an ivory handle. Ben knows the scales have tipped. His mind clouds with the horrors of what that knife must have seen and done, and he does his best to block the sinful visions out. The woman drops the bag and sharply drags the blade across the palm of her left hand, splitting the flesh and drawing blood.

'Dabo meum sanguinem, nam quid oporteat fieri!' she curdles, as she squeezes her left hand into a fist. Blood pours out of the bottom of her clenched palm. She raises the same left hand over her head, and shakes it like a salt shaker, raining droplets of hot fresh blood onto her hair, face and clothes.

Ben can take no more - the child crying, the maniac baroness embarking on some weird ritual. He charges at the woman, head down like a rhino. He wants to charge her full force off the ground and up backwards into the fire. The woman swings the blade upwards, and Ben feels that burning, urgent sickness as the knife sears through the meat just above his left collarbone. He curses himself, as he knows it was his fault - he left himself wide open, and knows he has had a lucky escape. Blood spits out of the gash by his left shoulder, down his shirt. He steps back away from the woman, who has stepped left away from the fire. She spreads her arms wide, like Predator beckoning Arnie to 'come and get it'.

'Magis sanguis vobis!' she screams. Ben has no idea what she is saying, just that it is Latin. That freaks him out enough.

Ben brings his fists up, and adopts a combat pose. They circle each other.

'Ego semper conantur ut dans...' the woman offers. As Ben circles closer to the fire, he can feel the heat prickle his skin. He knows he must act defensively, until there is an opening. He sees the woman's right shoulder dip back slightly, which gives him the split second heads-up he needs to know she is about to strike. He charges, just as the baroness brings the knife up and forward at his chest. Ben pivots his waist to the left, opening his shoulders to face the blade as it whistles past his midriff, and he grabs the out-stretched arm with both hands. He spins so his back is to the woman, and throwing caution to the wind, thrusts his head back to unleash a mighty head-butt. The impact is horrible and Ben knows it - it hurts him a lot, but he hopes that enough damage has been done to the woman to slow her down.

Fat chance, Ben thinks, as he feels her teeth sink into the wound in his collar bone. There is no quit in her at all. He still has her arm, but the strength he feels in her is unlike anything he expected. It reminds him of the kind of adrenaline surges people experience when they are in extreme circumstances - in the ultimate moments of 'sink or swim'. It's a natural reaction, nothing to do with the mind. If it was to do with the mind, he had imagined that sports people would use it all the time to jump higher, swim faster, hit harder. This woman seemed to be in a constant state of it. The teeth chomp harder, and he wriggles free, and in doing so, he is forced to sacrifice his grip on the arm. They break, and they are back to square one, staring each other down. She has a nasty gash above her right eyes, which itself is already developing a serious shiner. Blood pours from her mouth, but he knows it's not hers. It's his.

'Sanguinem ex oppositione...' she drawls, blood spraying as she speaks.

The baby is still crying, and Ben wishes above all else for this horrible scene to end. He changes tack. Defensiveness hasn't worked - perhaps an all-out attack will surprise her and he will get the upper hand, he reasons. With that, he summons up all the rage he can, all the hate he can muster. He knows he shouldn't, and that it is a bad practice in combat, but he knows it is that brute rage and strength that will help overcome this unlikely she-beast. He runs for her, and unleashes a scream, hoping that it will add to her confusion. He diverts his run, so he can leap off one of the low benches to his left and give himself a flying attack. In less than a second he is airborne, coming down on the baroness - who herself brings her knife up to meet him.

The blade rips into Ben's right thigh, but Ben barely notices it, as he flies over the woman's left shoulder. As he falls, he brings his own left arm around the woman's neck under her chin. Ben knows that despite the lack of a plan, this is working out alright so far. From where he is, he can execute a quick smooth judo takedown. He bends forward, locking his left arm around the woman's neck, and ripping her backwards over his arched back. She topples, as the knife tinkles somewhere. She crunches backwards onto the floor by the fire, with Ben still behind her. He aims to make his next move the last move of the fight. He keeps his left arm tight around her neck, and brings both his legs around her torso, interlocking his ankles. He brings his right arm around her forehead to clamp her head in place, and contracts all his body at once - locking the baroness in a monster sleeper-hold. He lies back and squeezes with every ounce of his being.

Ben has been forced to use this move a couple of times, and he knows when he gets down to it, it's one that is very hard to beat. He grips and doesn't relent. The woman squirms, but his legs stay firmly locked. His right thigh burns from the fresh gash, but it seems manageable for the time being, as he starves the woman of oxygen. She starts to kick frantically and buck. It's not an aimless spasming, however, as Ben realizes she is trying to get closer to the altar. She's not doing a bad job of it either - Ben can't let go of any limb lest it weaken the sleeper hold. He has to keep squeezing and hope that she passes out before they can get to the altar. Ben doesn't know if the altar is sturdy - it looks ok, but he can't risk a stray kick sending the whole thing, baby and all, toppling into the pyre. But they are getting undeniably closer.

He is forced into action. He barrel rolls the woman onto her front, with himself still attached now on top of her back, as she is face down in the dirt. But that only gives the woman the chance to rise to her knees, which she sure as hell begins to do. Ben has to roll again, onto his back, but they are getting dangerously close to the fire now.

He throws his weight to his left, onto his back again, and this brings a blood-curdling, choked scream from the woman. He wonders what has happened to bring about such a response, but then he notices. He has rolled the woman's feet into the fire. He can see the

78

black patent leather of her shoes bubble and pop. Ben closes his eyes and squeezes, begging for the end. As awful as the scene is, he knows he has her now. The kicking and bucking continues, but there is a growing futility to it. An awful leather and flesh BBQ stench wafts up to Ben's nose. Sadly, the flesh part of the smell is not foreign, and it brings back nasty memories. The woman has stopped screaming, and the bucking has nearly stopped. Her body loosens in tension, and flops in his arms. His mind can't help but think the ridiculous phrase: 'I just choked out an old woman while her feet were in a bonfire'.

He let's go, and shoves the woman off him onto the floor - her feet still in the fire. He sits back and doesn't know what to do next. Pull the woman out, or leave her for the authorities. It doesn't look great for his record, burning an old woman's feet off. Oddly, it seems to him that chucking her whole onto the bonfire might not look as sadistic. It's a strange logic that doesn't sit well with him, but he knows it might be the only way to stop this woman from harming anyone else. God knows how much harm this woman and her flock has reeked across this quiet beauty spot, but he knows that if he puts her on the fire, there will be no chance ever for her to commit or incite another atrocity. He puts his arms under he shoulders, and throws her unconscious body onto the fire. He doesn't wait to see what happens, and turns straight to the altar.

He approaches the swaddling, hearing the crying and hopes to God the infant is ok. He peels back the top layer to reveal a naked, pink, sooty but intact baby boy. Ben thanks his lucky stars, and breathes out. He puts his hand on the boys chest, which slows the crying almost immediately. He has no idea what to do with children, so his gesture is purely an instinctive one. For the first time in a long time, he experiences happiness. Glee feels so foreign to him, it comes as a surprise.

Sirens drift from over the lake. He looks back through the trees, and can see the dim flicker of red and blue down below. Time to go. He looks at the child, knowing the child is now safe. If he were to leave now, the authorities will be here within minutes to take the child, he reasons - plus the fire will keep him warm until they get here. It won't be long before he is back with his father. He wraps the child again, and, with a gesture that surprises himself yet further, he plants a kiss on the child's forehead.

'Take it easy, kid.' he says.

And with that, he looks straight up to the inky abyss of the sky. He can see the North Star. His work here is done. The baroness is dead. He runs and dives into the tree-line before the police can spot him, and heads off in an easterly direction. Back to England, back home - away from one of the most horrible and unexpected scenarios even he, in his combat-warped mindset, could ever contemplate, imagine or survive.

CATCH 23

1

The trial had absorbed Ben from the start. It had been splashed all over the television, all over the radio, all over the red-top newspapers. The broadsheets had barely touched it, and that perhaps should well have been an indicator of things to come.

Despite all the posturing of the media, about how Terry 'The Turn-Up' Masters was as guilty as they come, with a rap sheet more extensive and weighty than most hardback novels, the man had walked free.

He had practically stood on the court steps at the end of the trial, and admitted his guilt to his part in the armed robberies of a series of East London jewelers. He hadn't been present at any, but they had tied him to them thanks to some sloppy circumstantial evidence. One of the robbers had failed to fully tuck the collar of a particularly garish Hawaiian shirt down the neck of his boiler suit he was wearing for the robbery, which was like a red flag for the CCTV police investigators. A quick scan across the CCTV in a five mile radius of the first crime scene, revealed that The Turn-Up's own son, Markland, had been wearing that exact same shirt on the morning of the robberies. He was ID'd wearing that shirt in Tesco, passing through Marylebone Station and, hilariously, on the street where his father owns a pub (The Old Tupenny). Ben reasoned that Markland must be, for want of a better phrase, thick as pigshit.

Now, Ben sits in a rented Mondeo, staring through the drizzle-specked driver's window, at the front door of that very same pub. He has kept his distance to about 100 yards, and sits normal and relaxed, pretending to browse half-heartedly through a newspaper. When he had rented the car, he had also rented a kids booster seat to help with his story - if anyone asked why he was was sat doing nothing, he could say he was waiting for his kid to come out of whatever posh kid activity comes to mind. He fancies going with 'piano recital' today.

He doesn't worry too much at all about being either recognized or quizzed. He has absolutely no connection to the Masters family, nor does he have any connection with any authority - well not anymore. If the Masters were to look him up, chances are they'd find that Ben was perhaps even more wanted than they were, and connected to crimes just as grisly. They'd also probably find that nice little caveat that now appears on any paperwork of an official nature relating to him: 'DISHONORABLY DISCHARGED'. Given how bad that sounds, Ben almost thinks they should look him up.

Ben hadn't been too bothered by the crime (nobody had been hurt). What had crawled under his skin was the fact that Masters Sr. had been so untouchable, despite the myriad of crimes that are widely attributed to him. This was the first time he had ever seen the inside of a courtroom, but it doesn't matter: a quick google search reveals in lurid detail a guilty verdict. His wikipedia entry is a menu of some of the most godawful murders the streets of London have ever seen, peppered with the most liberal use of the words 'allegedly', 'reported' and 'according to a source'. If the reports were to be believed (and Ben does believe them) then Masters has a horrible record for dismembering his competition, and distributing their remains to the rest of his opponents. It's a reign of terror that has kept a stability to the London organized crime scene, in that nobody dare step up to take on the Masters'. But it has also brought an unruly bloodshed to the city that nobody who has come in contact with it can ever forget. Innocents scared on the street, neighbourhoods in the vice of terror... The Masters' are bad news.

When it comes to business, oddly, Ben found that the internet was less forthcoming. He knew of the pub, but that was pretty much it. Which of course, left the usual unofficial avenues of business the modern London gangster tends to busy himself with, namely drugs, arms and intimidation. But he didn't have specifics.

Ben wasn't here to pass judgement on those crimes, moreover he found himself traveling to London based on one solitary line in Masters Sr.'s address on the court steps. He had stood there with a long cream jacket perched on his shoulders (unable to look more like a 70's New York mobster if he tried), and had been asked 'Are you pleased to be acquitted of the charges?'. Masters had stared back into the female reporter's face, then let his eyes lower lasciviously. It was stomach-churning to watch, as the bug-eyed old pervert took her in, his game of intimidation in full flow. When his eyes came back up, he smiled and drawled: 'It didn't take the jury long to realize that the true Prince of London is untouchable.'.

On hearing it on the television in his Travelodge hotel room in Monmouth, Ben had felt that grim revulsion rise. At that point in time, he had been fleeing a particularly nasty situation in North Wales - a situation he had been most happy to commit to the farthest point of his rear view mirror and leave there. The figurative bile had risen at this vile man on the screen, and Ben, in search of a purpose, suddenly had one.

On the baking streets of Afghanistan, Ben had left the best parts of himself. But he hadn't done it so that scum like Terry Masters could run a bloody rule over the capital of the country. He hadn't done it so that Terry Masters could boast about being teflon to the nation, despite the numerous crimes he is linked to. He hadn't done it to come back to this once great nation and barely recognize it. Suddenly, Ben had an interest. If the law couldn't touch Terry, then, as a fugitive of that same law, Ben surely could. Ben had rented a car and set off to the capital.

He had been waiting for a glimpse of Terry for 48 hours. Ben had managed to get hold of a copy of a book about London crime, which featured Terry on the odd occasion but alluded to him heavily in others. It was the author's one and only book. God know's where he is now. The book had said that Terry's secrecy was paramount, and his movements always discreet - save for the occasional moment of brashness used primarily as a reminder, as if to say 'I'm still here and you still can't get near me'. It strikes Ben that that seems to be directed at both Terry's competition and the authorities simultaneously. A goading... a gloating... For Ben, it rang like a 'come and get me' plea. And that's just what he set out to do.

Ben has covered the pub in it's entirety, and knows exactly the layout of the pub without ever having had to set foot inside. He's been on the roof before dawn. He's been in the alley at the back. He's looked through the downstairs windows. And today, as soon as he has definitive proof that The Turn-Up is inside, he's going inside for a quiet pint. Or at least it will start quiet. If he gets in there, and the numbers look alright, he intends to get his hands on that lowlife piece of gutter-waste and get a confession out of him. Ben checks the mic on the inside point of his right shirtsleeve cuff, right by the button - still there, still fairly unobtrusive. He checks the dictaphone in his jacket pocket, which is connected to the mic via his sleeve. Also perfect - batteries charged, levels checked. Argos had come up trumps. The idea is to press record, get in, and make conversation. He'll pretend to be hammered if he has to get those words, or he's also prepared to dish out a hammering if it means he gets those words on tape.

Ben's role at present is not one he is comfortable with, but has accepted. He knows he has no place in this society. He knows that this society would never respect him. Service men don't always occupy a high place in society post-army, let alone disgraced servicemen like Ben. However, despite himself, he can't find himself to turn his back on this society. At times he hates this society with a flaming passion, and is outraged at how much he has given with so little in return. But he can't not care for this society - he seemingly can never forgo it's protection. He has no idea why, but he will bleed for this society. He will give everything for this society.

For Ben, it is a horrible marriage, but at least he has made peace with it. He believes that the problems in society comes from it's influences and undercurrent. Case in point, the culture of fame and celebrity. And that has begot a sense of entitlement in society, that we all should seek the trappings of such a lavish lifestyle. Now people want to be somebody just because it appears that that's what everyone aspires to. The desire for fame has never been so fierce. It sickens Ben. Seeing these girls who want to marry footballers, with no interest to careers. Seeing these lads get caught up wanting to be on reality tv, because it gets you famous. It's hopeless, Ben thinks. He can think of hundreds of examples where society is being flushed down the bog in slow motion, each more garish and unsettling than the last.

Ben often sits and wonders why he feels he owes such a pitiful society his protection, and he wracks his brains solemnly. Then he remembers the badge, the name, the honour of his position (well, at the time) and the simple word: England. Dear England, with it's history so rich and it's democracy so febrile. Dear England, with it's green hills and industry. Dear England, with it's dear Queen. When Ben thinks like this, he chastises himself quickly for being so maudlin. The romance of England is long gone - all that remains is the broken-down shell of a once thriving empire, with a bickering government trying to steer a disenfranchised and disillusioned populous out of the cave of economic uncertainty and ever-growing debt. Some ideal to fight for that is.

Ben is quickly snapped out of his thoughts by a man tottering along in his rear view mirror. The street is very quiet, but this man wearing a black jumper and cream khakis, seems to fill it with his charismatic, jaunty walk. He ambles along at a fair rate, but looks very much like he is loving life. He might as well be singing 'Oh What A Beautiful Morning' as he goes, thinks Ben. Ben has a suspicion as to the man's identity, and it's a suspicion that is confirmed by a couple of small observations. The red-top rag under one arm... The sparkling earrings in the left ear only... The shock of unruly black hair (so black that only an obvious bludgeoning dye-job can be responsible for it)... It's him alright. Terry 'The Turn-Up' Masters.

Ben can't quite believe his luck, and checks his watch. 2pm. The pub has been open for a couple of hours this drizzly Friday afternoon, but Ben's hunch had been correct and here he is. Ben had believed that if you owned a pub, Friday nights would be one you'd often spend at your place of work, through sheer force of habit. Ben was convinced that at some point today, the man himself would show. And, as if by some glorious magic, here he is. Early, but Ben had hoped as much. The earlier the better - less people in the pub, less things can go wrong. Ben has learnt through painful experience that the best way to ruin a plan is clog it with an unpredictable drunkard. And a pub? Well, that sure has the potential to up the quota of unpredictable drunkards.

Ben changes nothing about his behaviour - he doesn't freeze, nor does he frantically spin round to get a clearer view of his target. Moreover, he carries on slumping (if that's even possible) in his seat just as relaxed as before. He closes his eyes, as if struggling to stay awake. He doesn't worry where Masters is going - there can only be one destination. The pub. As Masters nears the car, the whistling becomes audible to Ben - he can't make out the tune, but as an aficionado of detail, he will likely never forget it. The Turn-Up strolls past, ambling care-free like he is on holiday. It infuriates Ben - every day must feel like a quaint getaway when you've got the whole city under your thumb and you're as unimpeachable as the damn Queen.

Masters hops the curb, and wanders directly through the front door of the pub, with the swagger that only the landlord could bring. Immediately, Ben moves.

He opens the car door with no strict urgency, and locks it without any special attention. He starts for the pub, twirling the keys in his hand, just for a second - he hopes the overall behaviour will give the impression of a bloke who just really fancies an early pint on a wet Friday, and is very grateful for the opportunity. He decides, along with all else, that he quite fancies a pint himself, and that makes the charade of walking innocently into a pub all the easier to execute. A simple stroll to the front door along a quiet street ('too quiet?',

Ben ponders, but doesn't dwell on), and the front door is in sight. He does a quick mental prep session (namely whispering to himself 'Don't fuck up now...') and enters.

2

Inside, the pub is just as he imagined. The shell of the pub is the archetypal, hulking, inner-city drinking public house, the shape of tradition festooned with the trappings of time and changing trends. Within that same shell, is a dark sticky-floored boozer, all spit, sawdust and too many plasma televisions, all blaring Sky Sports News at an intolerable volume. He approaches the bar, across a central wooden dance-floor that looks like, judging from the sickly mass of assorted drinks stains splattered right across it, it has seen a great deal of action. Nobody appears to be about at all, but he sticks to his role of 'cheeky drinker who should really be in work'. As he gets to the bar, his senses kick in, pondering options and possibilities, confirming strategies and plans.

He feels there must be at least one weapon behind the bar, close to the cash register. Most fights break out over money. He spies the cash register at the far right hand side. Ben thinks that may well be too far right to protect the entirety of the bar, so he reasons there must be another one on the far left. After all, you don't get to the highest branch of London's gangster tree by being lazy when it comes to security, do you? Ben heads to that left hand side, with a plan in mind to establish where the firearms dwell. Exits are where he came in, and presumably through the kitchen. The bar itself is open plan, with seating areas sectioned off by wooden partition walls. No other exits. Ben convinces himself he won't need one. Might as well get started, he thinks. Make contact with a barman, get the ball rolling.

'Hello?' he shouts. 'Anyone about?'

He gives the request that jovial lilt, that kind of vocal exuberance that doesn't suggest anything other than 'happy fellow'. He waits. A door clicks somewhere, as Ben's eyes are drawn to the kitchen door to the left of the bar, and he waits with an expectance that he desperately tries to keep hidden from his face.

'Just after a quick pint, but if you're shut...' he follows up. That should have set the bar staff's expectations for the visitor before they even lay eyes on me, he thinks. The kitchen door suddenly swings open, and to Ben's amazement, in walks Terry 'The Turn-Up' Masters. He looks unhurried and relaxed. Ben presses on with his task, even though it feels like he might drop his guts. He was not expecting alone time with Masters - at any point.

'I saw the pub and wondered if I could get a quick pint? I should really be in work, but you know...' Ben asks, while wondering if he laid it on a touch thick. Up close, Masters looks different - too much plastic surgery, which, away from the TV cameras and in the real world, looks extremely peculiar indeed. With that ludicrous thatch of jet black hair over a face full of improbably shiny and smooth angles, he looks like a part-melted Jim Henson creation. However he smiles with genuine warmth.

'I know the feeling!' Masters counters. 'Of course, we are open. What can I get you?'

There is a vulnerability to Masters that seems to come from his appearance - deep down there are some insecurities that needed to be masked by that near-ridiculous surface. This vulnerability, this patter... Ben was prepared for a lot of things, but he certainly was not prepared for him being likable. So he keeps going.

'Brilliant, thank you! Well, I'm a bit of a real ale man, so what can you recommend?' Ben gestures to the T-bar and the pump-clips above. 'You appear to have quite the selection!'

'Most of this stuff is forced upon us by the brewery - you know how difficult the pub industry can be at times. Always trying to cut corners, and leveraging against landlords - you'd be forgiven for thinking that the brewery's were trying to run the pubs out of business!'

Ben laughs genuinely, catching himself off guard, then chastises himself inside. 'Jesus, Ben' he thinks 'Be careful.' Masters continues.

'Despite all the wishy-washy cat-piss we are sometimes forced to stock, I always manage to sneak one in that's my own choice, which we do with one of our local suppliers by the barrel.' With that, Masters takes a small glass from behind the bar and squeezes the pump handle on the end of the T-bar, pouring Ben a little taster, which he duly hands over. 'Give this one a little try'.

Ben takes it, while Masters stares at him with hope and expectance, like he genuinely hopes that his own personal beer selection will impress the stranger. Ben smells it, and takes the small measure in one gulp.

'That's very good,' Ben says. Masters smiles warmly, and begins filling a pint pot with that same ale. 'You may have me here all day at this rate!'

'You're welcome anytime.' Masters responds, and puts the pint on the bar. Ben thinks about the second firearm he was hoping to pinpoint, but is forced to acknowledge that Master's hasn't done anything at all to reveal it - if it's even there, in fact.

'What do I owe you?' Ben asks.

'My treat - it's nice to meet a fellow ale drinker' replies Masters.

At this point, Ben is left in no doubt how Masters is as respected as he is, and how he finds himself perched high as London's crime kingpin. He is extremely charming, with a manner that commands both respect and loyalty. Ben feels more than a touch seduced, but he knows why that is - Masters reminds Ben of his father. The kindly, respectful, pub-dwelling charmer who goes by the name of Frederick Bracken. Ben hadn't seen him in years, and his own reaction to Masters' character surprises him in revealing just how much he misses his father - or indeed a father figure. Ben raises his glass.

'To sneaky pints' he suggests.

Masters nods and smiles. Ben needs to get to it, and needs to make this quality alone time count for something other than a hearty chit-chat.

'Is it always as quiet as this?'

'More often than not,' Masters replies. 'We only really get the same old faces in this place, and even they are few and far between'.

'It's a shame. It's a nice place.' Ben has a nice sup.

'Is that why you've been parked outside it for the last couple of days?' Masters asks cooly.

Ben damn near spits his ale out, but manages to keep it down. He glances at Masters over the rim of the pint glass at his mouth. Masters stares back expectantly with exactly the same demeanour as moments earlier. If the question wasn't loaded with spiteful intent, you'd never know. Ben is faced with a moment where he fears he has made a grave mistake. He thought he had been so careful with his own movements so as to avoid detection. He now feels extremely foolish, and totally underprepared - and worse than that, he feels like he has been smoked out. He realizes he has been drinking for an abnormally long time, and he needs to recalibrate his thoughts and think on his feet. He lowers his glass, and decides to fight fire with fire - still wrapped in the amenable nature of the conversation so far. His objective screams at him from the back of his mind: 'Get that confession!'

'Frankly I wanted to meet you. And you gave me a chance.'

Masters gravitates slowly towards the left of the bar, under the pretense of cleaning a glass with a mucky dishrag. For Ben, it all adds to the notion that there is a weapon secreted over there somewhere.

'The cloak and dagger stuff suggests you've got it in for me. Is that so?' Masters asks, hopping up to perch on the counter at the back of the bar. Ben walks over to follow him to his position, remembering he needs to stay close for the microphone to pick up anything that comes out of Master's mouth.

'I was hoping to have a chat with you, and we'd see how it went' Ben responds.

'And how is it going, in your opinion?' asks Masters. This polite verbal sparring is so off-kilter, with it's undercurrents of violence and menacing sentiments wrapped in lexical fluff.

'It's been extremely pleasant so far, but I would imagine you're about to give me some bad news on that front.'

'It depends. You can categorize most people who want a word with me as either police, those looking for a favor, or those stupid enough to think they can have a pop.' Masters fixes him with a searching sideways glance that crawls right under Ben's fingernails and itches. 'Which one is it that you fall into?'

Ben drinks some more, wondering if he can keep the conversation in amiable territory. Masters' candour has unsettled him so much, he feels that he must have some backup plan ready and waiting to instigate at a seconds notice. The longer he can stop that from happening, the better.

'While you are procrastinating...' says Masters.

Abruptly, Masters' gets up and creaks the kitchen door open. Ben flinches hard, readying himself for a sticky situation... but all he can hear is an odd slapping and clicking. A lot of slapping and clicking, getting closer. Masters whistles loud and shrill. The door thuds and clunks, the slapping and clicking unmuffles and is somehow in the room, and suddenly, three pitbulls run around the side of the bar into bar area, claws clattering off the wood around Ben's feet.

Ben looks down at them, as they wander about sniffling and waddling. They are compact and muscular dogs, with huge under-biting incisors below crumpled fleshy faces. They behave excitedly, as if they've not been this side of the bar for a while. Ben is struggling to believe what a fool he has been here - wading into a dangerous mobster's pub with a microphone, an impotent swagger and jack-shit else.

'Alright... what can I help you with?' Masters asks, perching back onto the counter-top. Ben tries to stay as cool as possible, given that three nasty-looking dogs are sniffing around his feet.

'I saw you on television' Ben says. 'You were on the court steps.'

'Ah, yes. The camera adds at least ten pounds, I was shocked too.' Masters quips.

'I was more interested in what you were saying, not how you looked. Although, now you mention it, you did look like a dementia ward patient in that jacket.' counters Ben. He tips his glass to Masters and glugs. This was part of the initial plan, so nothing to worry about so far. Irritate Masters into spilling something either out of anger or through showing off.

'You liked that jacket? I'll tell you about that jacket...' Masters starts to smile. 'That jacket is a hand-me-down. The original owner, well, he was an old fellow who... was reluctant to share. I wore that jacket to remind him how to share.' Masters' eyes flick to Ben and bore straight through him. 'Or at least, his old associates will have seen such a gentle little reminder.'

Ben just stares back - so close to a confession of any kind, but nothing yet. If he dropped that off to the police, the audio would find the waste bin pretty soon after the play button had been hit. Nevertheless, Ben wonders what the real story is behind Masters' anecdote.

'Before you get antsy, and you get any more excited, just have a look at the table by the fireplace,' Masters instructs. Ben slowly twists his head, but doesn't know where he is supposed to be looking. '4 o'clock', guides Masters. Ben follows the instruction, and catches two eyes looking back at him, from beneath the table. There is a third duller eye, but he knows what that is -

the scope on a rifle. He nearly loses the contents of his stomach there and then. He can't see the man in the murk, but he can see that it is an old hunting rifle, and it is trained directly between Ben's eyes. All bets are off. Ben's earlier suspicions regarding Masters' involvement in arms dealings seem pretty much confirmed. Ben glances around for cover - there's pretty much nothing in the vicinity that would protect him from that. Nothing at all.

Masters speaks. 'You know why I know you are here for a reason? To anyone, man, woman or child, within a 3 mile radius, this place is off limits. I barely even lock the door anymore. I run the charade of a pub, with the TV's on and the pumps active, but really? You're in over your head.'

'Tell me something I don't know,' says Ben.

'You've been sat in your car for the last couple of days, that shit little Ford. You must think either you're something special or I'm mentally defunct, because do you think I don't know for one minute everything that goes on in this street, the next street, the street after that, the street after that, the sodding street after that?'

Ben is stumped. He was expecting a wily character, but nothing like this. He feels outsmarted, outfoxed and outplayed.

'Simply put, do you have anything to offer me? You've been gradually sticking your beak in here, and I'm not looking for new friends. So unless you've got something of value to me, I'll be doing away with you here and now. So... I'm listening.'

The true Turn-Up has been revealed. Ben senses the terror that so many people must have felt at the feet of the this man, but keeps it at bay through sheer disrespect. There is nothing Ben admires about this man, and that is becoming the tool that Ben will draw upon to achieve his objective. He despises everything about this man's success, and he intends to let Masters know it.

'I was in Iraq as a grunt. Later, I was in Afghanistan as a captain. I've seen jumped up little Napoleons like yourself before, in a lot of different guises but a lot more menacing than you. I've seen things that would make your eyes widen despite yourself. I could tell you stories that'll make you want to march over to your precious beer pump and pour yourself another and another and another until you forget you heard them. If you think I'm scared of a few dogs, a bloke lying on a beer stained carpet with a peashooter unsuited to the job and an old fellow who looks more like David Gest held over a match for too long, then you are extremely incorrect.'

Masters veneer doesn't waver - moreover, it appears that Ben may have accidentally activated an even steelier layer, as Masters' lip begins to curl in a cruel sneer.

'Those dogs at your feet. They have scant regard for your sob stories from abroad. They won't listen to you when your trying to justify your pitiful, pointless existence. However, they will listen to me when I tell them to rip your fucking feet off.'

Ben senses movement from the other side of the room, and whips around to check it. The sniper is up and moving, but he's not coming with attack in mind. He's actually hopping up onto the bar, off the floor. As Ben notes that Masters himself is up off the floor, the penny begins to drop.

'Let's see what you're made of, grunt' Masters spits, then shouts 'Git! Git!' and whistles loud and long.

The dogs at Ben's feet look up, as if to smell the sound of the whistle. The dog on the left growls, a low throaty rumble through lots of teeth and saliva.

'Attack dogs were all the rage in the 60's. We used to train them and pit them against each other, and I never forgot the knack. The trick was finding a trigger and conditioning them with brute force. Batter them full of hate, that you can release with a simple whistle. Works a treat, even if I do say so myself'.

Ben looks at the dogs nervously, who are now circling him like squat fur-clad sharks. Ben gets into a crouch of his own, ready to fight tooth and nail just like the oncoming three might. He's never fought a dog before hand to hand, but he has had to get involved on a couple of occasions. Once, when he was in his teens, the family cat had got on the wrong side of a greyhound that was passing the front of the house with it's exhausted owner in tow. Ben had been sitting in the front room playing Playstation when he had seen through the window, the greyhound break it's leash and sprint breakneck at the poor bewildered cat. The cat had no chance, and the greyhound took it in it's mouth without problem. Ben ran out, and got his hands on the greyhound, but he just could't get the dog to release the cat. The dog just stared at him, it's jaws locked tight as titanium. It was all a big game. The dog never broke eye contact with Ben, while it slowly clamped down on the cat, popping and cracking it's ribs one by one. And they say cats are mean, thought Ben. Ben tried with his own hands to force the jaws open, but couldn't do it for the life of him. He gave up, and as soon as that happened, the dog didn't see the point in the game anymore. Ben had had to finish the cat off to put it out of it's misery - it was a harsh lesson but one that did him good for the years to come.

The dog in the middle charged - head up, teeth bared, spit flying. Ben had no teeth to counter with (well, none that would make any difference), so he threw a punch. Same principles apply - humans, dogs, it's still in incoming target. As his fist sailed through the air he had no idea how it would work out.

As it turns out, it works out pretty horribly. He manages to strike the mutt on the collar, and actually cuts his knuckles on the silver buckle. The force of the hit manages to send the dog sideways, so at least, for Ben, it's a start. The other two dogs are on him. The left one has a mouthful of trouser leg and shin bone, while the one on the right is airborne like the last. Ben swings his right boot into the dog clamping his leg, and makes good contact that doesn't even shift the muscular hound. The flying dog clamps onto his right arm, and bites hard. It is absolutely excruciating, and as the dog swings down still hanging, it feels to Ben like the most awful wet Chinese burn imaginable. He limps to the bar with the two dogs attached, raises his right arm with the dog dangling and swings the dog down onto the t-bar as hard as he can. The dog clatters, smashes and yelps as it releases it's grip and tumbles behind the bar. 'I hope that felt as ugly as it looked', Ben thinks.

The other dog has now joined the other in ripping his left calf to bits. Ben bends down and unleashes a hail of punches on the pair, left and right, left and right, all across the back, head and hindquarters. Nothing budges them. Ben can feel the flesh of his leg being shredded and separated. He grows increasingly desperate. He bends and twists himself as he does, so that he is practically straddling the nearest dog. He reaches for both the dog's front feet, grabs hold, and yanks up to the ceiling as hard as he can. Disgustingly, the dog's legs follow, and crack loudly as they too point at the sky in an improbable and fatal angle. He has ripped the dogs ribcage apart, and he didn't enjoy it one bit. The stricken dog slumps. It will be a horrible death for this one, and Ben takes no pleasure at all in it. The last remaining dog lets go almost immediately at seeing the fate of it's broken comrade, and backs away.

Ben stands there, his leg shredded and bleeding, with a gurgling, dying pitbull at his feet. He looks up at Masters, as if to say 'You were saying?'. Masters own face splits with rage, and he leaps off the counter whistling as he goes. The gunman rushes over, with a shocked look on his face too. It's a face that Ben recognizes - Markland, Masters' son.

The last remaining mobile dog careers around to what must seem a safer side of the bar. Masters is apoplectic, fizzing and frothing at the affront.

'Take out his knee' he orders his wingman. 'His left knee, split it.'

'Now?' Markland asks, agog.

'Yes, fucking now!' Masters bellows.

Ben looks for cover, sensing that the Markland's moment of indecision may be the only respite he gets before the bullets start hailing.

'But it's the middle of the day! Anyone could...' Markland remonstrates.

'Jesus christ!' Masters bursts. He's had enough. Inaction isn't something he is familiar with, so he rips the rifle from his son's grip and trains it on Ben.

'You. Stand still, and take a bullet through the knee, or I'll put one in your chest then two in your head. I've got further plans for you, but you're not getting away with that without getting shot somewhere. Either way you are going to die. I'm giving you a choice as to when.'

Ben stands stock still. Not much of a decision, when he thinks about it. Later will give him chance to assess a better chance of escape - he realizes now that escape is the only thing he can really hope for now, and leave Masters to his own devices. A choice with two awful consequences, no matter what he chooses. Ben has a survival instinct that just will not let him take or accept death - it is just not in his nature - so he loosens his shoulders, moves to the nearest table in the bar, and hops onto it. He points to his left knee, and lies back on the table.

'I will not forget this' Ben mutters to Masters, who appears surprised by the decision. He takes hasty aim. Ben shuts his eyes, grits his teeth, and waits. He has been shot before, but that time he didn't expect it, and the impact of it had shocked more than the pain. Now, as he leans back and waits for what can only be insufferable pain, he realizes the waiting is worse.

'You stupid, stupid prick' says Masters.

The gunshot is louder than Ben expected, a bright, deafening crack. The shock of the noise almost masks the impact of the bullet, but the pain it brings is absolutely immeasurable. He has been shot just above the knee, in the fleshy plateau at the base of the thigh. Masters clearly isn't that great a shot. Ben knows he has had a lucky escape in a way - that rifle should have ripped his knee to pieces with a direct hit, so much so that he'd probably be a touch lucky if there was anything left below the knee. That's not to say it doesn't hurt. It is an awful searing pain, like a burning icepick has been smashed into his flesh with the point left inside. It is a dizzying, vile, sickly pain, that brings an instant fever to Ben's brow. He feels his grip on consciousness loosening, and begins to slip into a figurative black abyss. As he slumps onto the table, signing off temporarily, his last thought is one of wondering just what he will wake up to, and what horrors they will do to him while he is out of it.

3

Ben is awakened by his sense of smell - the first of his senses to return as his body reboots to lucidity. An acrid, musty, moldy, coppery smell is dragging Ben into the present, and he resists. What had forced him into unconsciousness was so awful, so painful, he really doesn't want to see what faces him when he wakes. But that smell - it's such an interesting concoction that it demands his attention, and piques his interest.

But, another sense is sharpening and with it comes the pain. Ben remembers. He remembers being shot, he remembers Masters' smug bastard face, remembers the awful choice he was forced to make. Die now or die later. Great, he thinks. What with the stench and the returning pain, he is forced to question his own prior decision. He senses his left arm feeling a bit funny. A bit numb. He forces his eyes to open, so he can address this godawful situation.

First, off, it's dark. Not pitch black or anything, but dark enough to be a bit sinister and very disconcerting. Ben sees shafts of turquoise light piercing from above, down onto a wet, puddle-strewn metal floor, and as his eyes adjust, he sees he is in a dank, metal-clad room somewhere. He tries to sit up, but it's not easy - his balance is off, and his torso feels strange. Stretched, pulled, tight. His range of movement isn't the same - not painful, just inhibitive. He looks down. His red shirt (that old thing) is ripped to pieces, wide open. His chest and stomach is bare, and slick with blood and that dirty stinking water.

And then he notices his left arm is missing. He panic for a moment, but it's only for a second as he realizes that it is actually strapped behind his back. His panic subsides, as he examines the binding with his right hand. It feels like a belt around his left wrist attached fast to his own belt. Confusion seeps and he tries to claw at the buckle on his wrist.

'Behave yourself', a voice blares, bouncing off every surfaces, tinnier with every resonance.

Ben snaps round, and there he is - Masters. Brooding in the darkness, dressed exactly as before, but flanked by four burly besuited men that Ben has never seen. His heart sinks, but he knows he shouldn't have expected a ticker tape parade. His instincts hone for an exit, but he knows its useless and doesn't even bother. One against five and that's at the optimistic scale of things. Ripped up by dogs, shot in the leg, one arm tied behind his back... it's bad whichever way Ben contrives to dress it up. But it's the purpose of this that Ben is even more nonplussed by. The vindictiveness with which Masters set his pitbulls on Ben, suggests that not much is off the menu as far as what he is willing to do in terms of retribution.

It turns out he doesn't have long to wait. Masters throws something onto the floor in front of Ben, which tinkles and glints in the aquamarine phosphorescence. A kitchen knife. Somehow, Ben's heart sinks lower. Masters smiles grimly and folds his arms.

'Do him' he orders, cocking his head to Ben's right. Ben follows the gesture - to see another equally doomed man, his left arm strapped behind him also. He looks largely untouched, but, nevertheless, extremely agitated. He stands, a bit like a scolded child, waiting for instruction. And it hits Ben that indeed this man is a child - Masters' own child. His son, the gunman from before. His eyes leak betrayal, and he looks like he may have filled his trousers at Masters' words. Ben looks back at him, and roots around in his larynx to find his voice.

'I knew you were a piece of shit, but this...' he croaks.

Masters tightens his grimace.

'You've disrespected me with your so-called balls of steel all day. I don't get it. I don't get it at all. I've been in my little bubble, you've been in yours - co-existing blissfully on our own terms. And your drop out of the sky with an iron-clad problem with me. You've decided your going to come into my house and piss on my drapes. You come at me with a fucking wire trying to dupe me into spilling something, so you can make a little name for yourself. Do you think this is the first time I've been around the old oak tree?'

Masters reaches in his pocket and pulls out the dictaphone, wires rapped around a central object, and he holds it out. It gives Ben, oddly, the impression of someone having disemboweled a robot, as Master's flings it loudly to the floor.He continues. 'I can't tell you how much this has... offended me in the deepest pit of my stomach. I also can't tell you what awful things have happened to people who have done so much less than what you have done.'

Ben sighs.

'Are we going somewhere with this? It's been a long-arse day.' Masters seethes at that, and Ben takes a minuscule bit of heart that he has managed to get right under the scumbag's skin like that. Masters points a quivering finger at his son.

'He has let me down unforgivably. That dicking about in that pathetic shirt all over town was bad enough... What it led to was heartbreaking. My own son's spluttering thickness got me in court - for the first time. Had to buy the judge and jury, I mean it wasn't a problem, but overall I'd have preferred not to have been dropped in it by my own bloody spawn. But then... that gibbering over pulling the trigger. Untrustworthy. I can't forgive him. And I can't forgive you. Hence your current predicament.'

111

Ben glances again at the knife, and then at Markland, who has risen from his knees and stares imploringly at his father. Ben finds it doubly horrible - on one hand, it's awful watching this father-son relationship crumble and dissolve so sickeningly, and on the other hand, Ben dreads the prospect of actually having to harm Markland. It would feel like wounding a puppy.

'I'm telling you, to do him in. There's a knife there - it should be easy. But I want to make you sing for your supper. Let's see how much you both want it. How much you both want to survive. I know you've got a keen survival instinct - mopping up my fucking dog showed me that - so I'm sure that's no problem for you. I want to see how much my son wants to survive. And I want you to make it hard for him. Make him go that extra yard to prove he's got some kind of point. And you get the knife first because I don't think you want to do it just for shits and giggles, whereas I think my son, the dopey shit, will do whatever he can, bare hands and all.'

And before he's got his last word out, or before Ben can respond, Markland has sprinted to the knife and clasped it tight. Ben doesn't move - he genuinely doesn't feel that much threat from Markland, with or without a knife. He is banking on the notion that nepotism has been Markland's loyal friend, right the way through his life. He wonders if he ever got his hands dirty at all. Judging by the way he is holding the knife out at Ben, raised so high he might take his own jugular out, Ben guesses 'not likely'.

'Well, that's a good start' Masters smirks.

Ben rises to his feet but it causes fissures of pain blazing above and below the bullet wound in his leg, and the movement is a grim sickly one which brings jagged sparkles to his eyes.

Markland takes two steps forward, the knife still so high that it annoys the hell out of Ben. 'What are you going to do with it like that? You look more like Bob Ross than Andy McNab. Holding it more like a sodding paintbrush than something to end someone with. A knife is an intimate tool for an up-close and personal death. Anyone can pull a trigger, but can you push a knife into warm flesh?' he thinks.

Markland makes a short sharp lunge, that stinks of half-commitment, as he tries to find his range. Ben sidesteps it easily without his pulse even rising one bit. He is desperate to get his hands on Masters, and looks for an opening. If he can get the knife, even for a split second, he might be able to throw it at Masters. That'd make the old bastard blink, he thinks. While he doesn't recognize the threat from Markland, he certainly doesn't want to disrespect the knife. The knife doesn't care whose holding it. If there's something to pierce, it will. He keeps his eyes between the knife, Markland's right shoulder, and Markland's panic-strewn eyes. He'd like to add a fix on Masters to that trifecta, but he can't just yet.

Markland jabs again, and Ben blocks with his right arm with ease. There was a bit more juice in it this time, and that focusses his attention once more. Ben decides the sooner this is over, the better - and then he can get back on to his real quarry. He feints left at Markland, drops his head, and sends an uppercut with his right - which misses. Markland, in his livewire state, might have a move or two in him yet. Ben bobs back, but not so far as to show too much respect, but then immediately moves in again at top speed. The torque flexing through his wounded leg as he moves is extremely painful, but he's had worse. He may face darker battles later if he survives this ordeal, with all this stinking, reeking water sloshing about in his open wounds.

He makes hard contact with Markland - chest to chest. It is a primal move, and one that does little except illustrate warring authorities between scrapping males. The shock of the move gives Ben the opportunity to make a play for Markland's knife, which he reaches for with gusto. Markland keeps the knife away from Ben as fiercely as possible, like an overzealous child refusing to share candy. Ben keeps pressing against Markland's chest, forcing him backward while they both scrabble at the knife in Markland's hand - when Markland trips.

He falls backwards, with Ben falling atop him. A sharp exhalation of breath and a deep thunk tell Ben what has happened without him even needing to look. In the melee, the knife has plunged into Markland's chest. Ben looks up, and sure enough, the knife is buried in Markland's sternum, with Markland's face belying shock, but crucially, no pain. He is frozen in shock, and Ben knows that look a mile off. Markland's heart has been irreparably punctured. It's not the gasping wheeze of someone whose lung has been punctured, nor the searing agony and writhing that follows an intestinal piercing. Moreover, its the cold result of a fatal tear to the heart. The end for Markland is extremely close.

Ben didn't mean it. He had hoped that he wouldn't have to kill Markland at all - rather that seeing his father getting his just desserts would stop him just as easily. It's one nasty accident, and one that will result in this dolt losing his life. Ben swings round to where Masters Senior was stood before, but the room is empty. He spins his head left and right, but indeed, nobody is there - the shadows are bare. Ben knows that pulling the knife out won't make a difference, but he needs it to get free. He reaches down to Markland, and places his knee down on his chest, pressing down to enable freedom of the knife with a sharp upward tug. It works, but the result is horrible. The knife slick with bright crimson, which springs forth geyser-like. Markland just stares at the ceiling, breathing shallowly.

Ben uses the knife to free himself, and suddenly he has use of both arms again. He keeps the knife, in case he can catch up with Masters - who knows what he might need to get the job done if he can reach his prey.

He heads for the shadows, to find an exit, as his eyes adjust to the darkness, but all he finds are metal walls. Before confusion and panic can eke in and take hold, a voice breaks right through the quiet chamber.

'Freeze!'

4

When it dawns on Ben where he was, he can't quite believe it. He wasn't surprised when the police appeared, even though he wasn't thrilled. He had been expecting them right from Manchester, through North Wales, and then all the while on through his recent sojourn to the Big Smoke. Finally seeing a copper was almost a relief. He hand't been surprised when he was cuffed and told that he was under arrest, for a range of crimes including murder. He was holding a knife that he had just pulled from a dying bloke's chest - not that much of a stretch to join the dots there, even if the police didn't know the true circumstances.

No - Ben was surprised when the police led him out of the room, via a clanking metal door in the back right corner, and into another putrid, eroded corridor. They escorted him along the corridor, up a flight of stairs, and into another corridor, each turn revealing something just as decayed as the last. A final left turn had brought them out onto the bow of a ship. This had literally caught Ben's breath. As he walked to the hastily erected exit plank, he saw that he was standing on an abandoned boat moored on the banks of the Thames, with the London Eye itself looming overhead, casting a cascade of halogen on the surreal scene.

Sadness sets in, as he is greeted on the banks of the Thames by tactical support units, ready to take him down on the tiniest instruction. He is abruptly cuffed, while he looks back at the boat. He still can't shake the surprise, and can't help but feel akin to the stricken vessel. A piece of great use and worth, strewn to one side and abandoned by those who had promised to care for it, now only fit for dirty work. As he is led into the back of the armored transport, and the ambulance teams run onto the boat to get something out of Markland, Ben is further crestfallen. Masters has disappeared, and Ben's own capture can only be viewed as his own fault. He had tried to take on a target too big, too powerful, and he was underprepared with a poor plan. His heart had ruled his head, on this occasion and the last few months overall. He only ever tried to do the right thing, but it has resulted in a pretty hefty rap sheet. And it's a rap sheet that, as he is chained to the inside wall of the van and it's doors are slammed shut, may ensure he doesn't see the light of day ever again - and he only has himself to blame.

THE THINGS WE CAN'T UNDO

1

The day is so drab that it barely warrants description. A wet grim-grey that can only mean one thing - urban England in November. Rain pats softly on the street, in that half-arsed way that still somehow manages to get you soaked through. Nothing of any note whatsoever, save for the spirals of barbed wire that surround the building at the end of the street. Huge blocks of brickwork peppered with soft halogen complete the look, not to mention the high walls that surround the edifice - designed to keep the in from the out and vice-versa. An imposing structure that stinks of discipline - Strangeways Prison, Manchester.

A recessed door in one of the high walls clunks open, and some people file out into the drizzle. Mostly women, a couple of burly blokes, and one old fellow - about twelve in total. As soon as they hit the street they disperse, no joy anywhere to behold. The two big men catch up with each other, and head off up the road. The others slink off glumly - back to their lives, which are probably broken thanks to the actions of those they just visited. The older gentleman heads down the street directly to a car parked on the side of the road. He has the usual grey hair of advanced years, but carries a height and stockiness that belies a past where this man stood tall and vital. He approaches the car, beeps the keyless entry, and climbs in the driver's side.

Behind the wheel, he takes a second. He had driven a couple of hours to get here, to make the morning visiting hours, and it is catching up with him a bit. He unzips his coat and, from the breast pocket, pulls out a white envelope. There is a name on the front, and an address, neither of which he recognizes. The man he had just seen asked him simply to post this for him. He said he didn't trust the letter to get out if he put it in the usual letter boxes inside the prison walls. The man hadn't elaborated, he just said he preferred it to be taken care of by anyone else.

The old man doesn't know the prisoner very well, but knows the kind of man he is. He has seen his kind many times before, but this man has something different. A resolve, a steeliness - that is bound tight by mental darkness. A girder dropped down a desolate well. There is something about the prisoner that made the old man want to visit, to want to lend a hand. Much of it can be down their similarities, he supposes. But the prisoner has asked him to do something, something he is not completely sure he should do. The old man knows too well, that heated actions rarely have positive consequences, and he desperately doesn't want the prisoners life to worsen thanks to even more poor choices. The old man feels he must open the letter, although he is not sure whether it's out of trying to do the right thing or to satisfy his curiosity. Either way, he feels his finger slipping into the envelope and tearing it open, before he had even decided whether or not he was going to do it.

He pulls out a few sheets of lined paper, folded neatly thrice. Handwriting all in block capitals. Dag's eyes flit across the first few words, and he already knows he will read this document to the end.

2

"Dear Kayla,

This letter is one that I never expected to write, and I'm sure is one that you never expected to receive. I suddenly find myself with some time on my hands, and it has forced me to address elements of my past that I have put off for far too long. My intention, in the long run, is to become a better man and to set the record straight. Please indulge this note and consider the contents, because I feel it is important that you hear what I have to say. I always hoped I'd be able to tell you this in person, but I may never get the chance, and that brings us to where we are today. My name is Ben

Bracken - it may not be a name you recognize. You know me better as the man who killed your husband.

As a prologue to what is to follow, please can I tell you that not a second passes without the weight of what happened pressing down on every inch of me. It informs every decision I make, gnaws at every part of me, and drives me sleepless long into the night. I can't shake it. I hope by the end of this note you will understand a bit more, but let me please get another thing straight. Be under no illusions. I'm not writing to you asking for forgiveness - I'm not a man who deserves that. I'm writing to you for two reasons. Firstly, I feel you should know the truth, and secondly, it feels like, after all this time, the right thing to do.

From the outset, I will promise a few things. Blunt honesty is one of them. I'm not renowned for being much of a fantasist, nor am I a man who will embellish unduly. I will tell it like it was, and I will try not to leave anything out. Another thing I will promise is my regret. In case it doesn't come across in my written words, my mind is sodden with regret for what happened. If anything sounds too blunt or matter-of-fact, that is me 'the soldier' speaking. Me 'the human being' struggles with guilt full-time. My final promise is that after this note, I will never contact you again. I'm gambling on it reaching you, but I don't want anything in return. Not a thing. But you will know the truth, and that is my only concern.

I'm going to pretend that you know nothing of the events leading to your husbands death, so I will give you the facts as I know them and experienced them. You may have been fed a pack of lies, for all I know, so please let's start afresh.

I met your husband after I'd been at Camp Bastion for a couple of months, very soon after it's opening in 2006. I had recently been promoted to Captain, and your husband had been added to my squadron after my previous communications officer finished his final tour (that's no metaphor or euphemism - he literally had finished all his schedule tours of action and was destined to return to the UK).

Steven (even writing his name is difficult) arrived, but unlike most other newbies, he was comfortable with his calling, and eager to learn. He wanted to be the best of the best, and to give him his credit, he was indeed excellent at his job. He was a wonderful addition, and I was very glad to have him. He had an enthusiasm and matter-of-factness that made him great to be around.

Something that soldiers judge each other on timelessly, is the ability to act under pressure. Some greenhorns simply hear the word 'hostile' in their earpiece and frankly, shit their pants. Everything they've ever learned goes out of the window, and they are more like baggage when it comes to a pressure situation. If you can imagine being smothered under enemy fire and having a six foot toddler with you, you kind of get the idea. This was never the case with Steven - he was alert, composed and well-drilled. He looked like a born soldier, which is a ridiculous cliche that gets overused whenever the newspapers pen a hasty obituary. I never read Steven's so it may be in there.

He was popular with the men in our unit, and very quickly so. He was immediately reliable in the field, and people latched onto him like a beacon in a storm, but it was his human side that people really gravitated towards. On an army base, thousands of miles from home, with genuine combat always near-present, at times it can feel a bit like a psychiatrist's waiting room out there. People wandering about in an uneasy state, agitated, nervous, scared, pumped, stressed - it was a gala of warring emotional states at times. Steven's cool head and easy ear elevated his status and respect quickly. People sought him out for a chat, or to get his take on things. He almost became a resident agony aunt. Throughout this period he became one of my very best friends.

In addressing where I was at this point, I was a man who was emotionally impermeable. I had shut down that facet of me, as my military persona had grown. I saw psychiatric weakness or softness like a huge crack in a wall - a point of weakness which the enemy could exploit to let the pain rain in. I had plastered over that crack as thick as I could, and would not let anybody in. Steven saw this and, with no fuss whatsoever, and with no ill-intentions, eased me open like an oystercatcher would a clam shell. I resisted at first, but Steven later told me he could see what being that way had done   to me. I was a resentful, hateful mess. I was livid at life. I was single-minded and brutish with scant regard for the joyous variation life has to offer. I was the perfect soldier, but a far from perfect man.

It started over a quiet beer in the pub tent. Bastion had an array of fast food outlets (including a McDonalds and a KFC, if you can believe that) but I always fancied something a bit more home-cooked. If was going to be fighting for England, I felt I might as well eat like it. So we found one of the tents was set up more like a village pub feel, and felt myself naturally gravitate there. Years prior, I spent hours and hours of my infancy on the floor around my fathers swaying feet, which dangled off whatever barstool he happened to be perched upon. I used to count the ridges on the contours on the soles of his boot. I taught myself to tie and untie shoelaces. Occasionally nuts and crisps would be passed down to me. It felt an extremely happy period, but on reflection I was little more than a loyal dog. But like a loyal dog, I was happy, so I hold no resentment. As an adult, I now cling to pubs like they are a much-welcomed oasis. An island of calm.

We had a beer and this lad in my unit cut right to the core of me. He said he could see that there were murky clouds over my head which were mopping up some kind of sadness, but that it was this same sadness that was stopping me from moving forward in life. I never took leave - didn't want it. I wanted to keep my head down and lose myself in the fight. I was well decorated, and a successful soldier. But out in the real world, that counted for very little - but it was my focus.

The truth is, Kayla, that above the veneer, shrouded in a haze of booze, faux-pride, combat-hardened exoskeleton, I'm an utter sham. I use whatever I could to build a moat around my fragile centre, and Steven saw this. I have always been a man riddled with principles arranged in jet black and ice white - but there was a time when these principles were eroded and somewhat blurred. I met a girl once, in 2002. In a nightclub. I was still at Sandhurst, and I was on weekend leave, and had come back up to Manchester for the weekend to see the folks and sink a few jars.

With some of my old school friends, we ended up over near Canal Street. It was a good night and all, and we were in this gay bar. I had never had a problem at all with other people's sexual choices - and in any event, contrary to popular belief, the army kind of smashes that kind of unimportant navel-gazing out of you. It's of no consequence what side of the sexual fence you reside. In hostile territory, anybody wearing the Union Jack is your friend. There was a girl there who I can only assume was accompanying her gay friends. Again, this was all very normal - in fact it was one of the reasons we used to go there sometimes. You used to be able to meet the odd nice girl in the gay district who was there with her friends, too timid to go off by herself. I know that sounds terrible, and illustrates us as rather predatory, but it wasn't anything like that.

I met Steph there that night, and was very smitten right away. My exterior crumbled, the army man in me both fighting off the attack of desire, while the regular joe in me simultaneously harbored, and urged it to blossom. For a simple bloke, it was a dangerous concoction. We hit it off in a nuclear way. I would come back to see her 5 consecutive weekends in a row.

We were in contact during the week too, when she wasn't working or I wasn't training. And it was in one of these conversations that she told me - she was pregnant. The floor fell out from under me. I was horrified, uncertain, hurt, frightened, shocked, despairing - but above all, I was delighted. My world was assigned a meaning aside from the army. A purpose I had not predicted or foreseen, yet certainly didn't realize how much I would welcome. I didn't know how delighted I had been until the very next conversation we had, two days later. She told me that she had "got rid of it".

We both acknowledged after a long, tumultuous conversation that it was probably for the best, and that we were in no fit state to raise a child. We barely knew each other - never mind that, we barely even knew of each other. We never spoke again after she ended the call and I listened to the static hiss of rejection on all fronts. I realized I had been listening to that same crackle for 10 minutes before I came to my senses and hung up.

I was at sea with clashing emotion. The decision may well have been the right one, but surely, as co-producer of whatever creation adorned her womb, I was entitled to be a part of the decision? I could see a future ahead of me, that I would never know. It's like a fork had been placed in the road of my future and I had been forced down one of the roads, while so close to the other, I could visualize it. I could feel it. I could feel parenthood.

No non-parent will ever understand this. A funny switch flicks deep inside an untouchable recess in you, and a torch is lit forever, as a connection with your child is created. It doesn't matter if the child is embryonic or fully borne - that sense of purpose, protection, duty and LOVE is overwhelming. It changes everything about you, but also crystallizes your very essence at the same time. It makes you a person. It gives you a reason.

Perhaps it's because, as humans, we are built to procreate, and by creating children, we are therefore fulfilling our own point of existence. But that feels like it would cheapen the dizzying euphoria, and blunt the searing point of excited purpose. My own excitement was short-lived. No sooner had I been given the almighty news that I had created life, but that same life was taken away from me.

Imagine, for a second, being given a purpose and then having it stripped away from you before you even had the chance to experience it or were allowed the exhilaration to set in. But even saying that withers the weight of the utter crushing sorrow that came next. My child, was taken from me. Killed. Poisoned, and flushed away. I will never forget the bitter taste of hate I felt after the shock had subsided. I taste it every time I think about it. I'm gagging on it now. My mouth fills with it every time I see a child in any kind of danger. I sometimes cannot read the paper without wanting to spew venom-specked bile all over it.

I'm waffling. I know this. I'm sorry for the filibuster, but, in a selfish way, this may prove hugely helpful. Steven helped me with this so much before... But even as I ramble, I know I am struggling to get around to the nitty gritty, and as I feel it loom ever closer, anything and everything feels like a better topic. But I know that isn't helping you at all. In fact, if you have read everything in this letter leading to this point, you have done everything I asked when I first started writing - and I'm grateful. So, without further ado...

Loosely, but also oddly succinctly, we were caught up in an awful situation involving a murder hole. 'Murder hole' is a particularly vicious expression, but the reality is worse, I promise you. They are almost mythical in stature within the infantry, and ground excursions are always all the more tense because of them. Simply put, think of a house on a street. Now, in that house, think of the wall that faces the street - think of a hole in it, through which you can poke the barrel of a gun and point it indiscriminately at the street. You can't see what you are aiming at, but you can see the crowd, the rush of people, and the occasional flash of British army camo. That's usually enough to act. Murder holes are the perfect way to satisfy a lot of urges - none of them good - but if you are a Taliban fighter with a shot at a prize scalp, this is a very safe way of doing it.

As the guy on the ground that may be wary of a murder hole, it's a seriously unsettling experience. You can't see them. You can't hear them. You can't feel them. But then there's a pop and a spit of gravel, as the muzzle bucks in the hole, and someone in your vicinity goes down. And that person that goes down is rarely the intended target. I've seen women and children become the victim of this more often than I'd care to mention. The aftermath is dreadful, and the worse thing is, you can't find it. You can't find the hole to stick your own barrel down - for a hundred reasons. Too much is happening, there's a civilian down, or a comrade is hurt, more bullets are hailing from that same tiny somewhere, and, let's face it, we are talking about a war torn environment. There are hundreds of bullet holes, cracks and faults in the walls on your average street, and the last thing you want to do is stick the pointy end of an assault rifle down the nearest one and spray an innocent family's living room full of hot metal. All you can do is get down and get away - as fast as you can.

Steven was indeed the victim of a murder hole, in a way. We had been on a dusk excursion across the province via air, when our Apache was hit with a small volley of bullets. They pinged and whizzed only briefly, the air in the cabin spitting hot poison for a split second, but a cruel ricochet within the cabin sent a stray bullet through the copilot's visor. He buckled and fell forward, across the central controls. At that time, it was probably the most unlucky casualty I'd ever seen in combat. The helicopter went down fast, as we struggled to get the copilot off the column. Whoever fired the shots made himself a hero. One man with a peashooter, essentially, took down one of Her Majesty's prize eagles. It should not have happened, but fate has a strange way of spinning you a rum one.

As we went down, our perspective shifted as the chopper angled onto it's side. As I looked out of the open window, all I could see was faces watching. We fell into a crowd of people - a busy evening market scene was disrupted by 18,000 pounds of twisted metal. We hit a building as we fell, which slowed our descent. It saved my life - and Steven's. It pitched the falling tin can upright, nose pointing to the sky, and we were saved because the impact threw us. It jolted us out, and we dropped 10 feet to the tarmac. Another twist of fate - everyone else was strapped in. We were lazy, and weren't. We fell out and they stayed in - which wasn't much use when it went up in eager flames.

The crowd fanned as we dropped and rolled, narrowly avoiding the falling chassis of the chopper, and all the other rags of blazing hardware that were dropping from above. We weren't unscathed at all - I had a series of cuts in my scalp, so that even now when I shave my head, my hair grows back in a giraffe-style patchwork until it gets long enough. My right ankle was, if you'll excuse the vernacular, fucked. I would eventually find out it was fractured, but at the time I barely noticed it. Steve had a flesh wound to his chest, not too deep, but deep enough to really sting and scar. But aside from that, he wasn't in too bad a condition, and, considering he had just survived a helicopter crash, he looked remarkable.

We were out and away from the immediate crash site, but we couldn't stall - we knew the gunfire had come from this vicinity, and that, seen as hostiles, we were surely sitting ducks. A crowd was forming, and I could sense our safety becoming ever more compromised. Dizzy and disorientated, we headed away from the centre of this village as quickly as we could, trying to find the backstreets off the central drag.

As we stumbled along, keeping close to the walls of the street, trying to get our bearings amid the melee, there was a little, barely audible, spit. Like a gasp from somewhere, the Grim Reaper himself breathing sharply from the Netherworld, excited at the close-proximity of another soul to take. Steven stumbled, but we carried on moving - wobbling, whirling, two steps forward, two steps back. The hubbub of the crowd was growing, and distant gunshots began to echo. As we trawled the street, we noticed the entrance to a sewer, embedded in the dusty pavement. I levered it open with my rifle muzzle, and the stench wafted up to us from the murk below. For want of a better expression, the smell was a barrage of hot shit. It's seared into my nostrils, filling my sinuses with it's filth, so that now, I can't even drive through good old English countryside for fear of catching a whiff of something manure-like, and be transported back to the moment we dropped into that Helmland sewer.

As we landed in that infinite cesspit, the reek was unbearable. Steven was with me, and we both looked at each other to communicate one very prescient sentiment: 'We have to get out of here'. Looking up, through the sewer access grid, we could see the purple sky we had fallen from. Glancing below... it was unspeakable. We started to move through waist deep water, that was thicker than normal water, and well... chunkier. Bits and pieces floating into my feet and hands, each time triggering a weakening gag reflex. I was wading, following the darkness, trying to put the unfriendly light behind me. I was throwing up as fast as I could take breaths. But as I trekked, I noticed that the distance between me and Steven was lengthening. For a couple of moments, I kept pressing, hoping that my pace would help spur him on. But it wasn't working. Worse, he was slowing. I dropped back to him, and asked how he was. He said he was fine, but thought he had pulled a muscle in his abdomen. This alarmed me immediately. Under pursuit from a lynch mob, I would have thought only about tearing my hamstring from the bone would slow me down, never mind a pulled muscle.

Then I remembered the gasp as we were on street level. That sharp fizz of air augmented by trajectory. I hauled Steven to the wall of the sewer, to lean him against it. I lifted him up so he could perch on a brick shelf about a foot above water level, which was just wide and strong enough to support his weight. I lifted his fatigues, and checked his stomach. Just next to his belly button, was a small dark purple hole with black edges of wet ragged skin - a little fleshy well. And sloshing into that well, was the sewer filth. I could literally see the detritus in and around the wound, and I began to panic. Our field packs were sodden with the unspeakable, and Christ knows what our first aid kits were swimming in. Cleaning that wound and getting our hands on some antiseptics became an urgent, all-encompassing priority. But we were, bluntly put, in a dark sewer underneath a swarming village filled with any and all who might like us dead - and to make matters worse, night was drawing in.

Steven asked what I could see on his stomach, and it seems completely ridiculous to mention it now, but I told him 'Nothing. You're good to go.' You know when a child falls down, or someone is in acute pain, and you tell them everything is OK, and that they are fine. There's a million reasons we do that, and it works both ways. We say it so that they don't worry, to ease in calming them down. For the person saying it, we are trying to hold onto something concrete and soothing while figuring out what to do next, even if the words represent a past that has recently been fundamentally altered - 'You're ok, you're ok (well, you were ok a couple of minutes ago, but know I don't know how we are going to get the care you need)'. There was no selfish inclination to me telling Steven that he was fine, other than to keep his spirits up and to keep doubt and fear from creeping in and taking vicious hold. Plus, I wanted him to keep thinking his body could function at optimum capabilities for as long as possible - we needed to move and if he started fretting about how bad the pain was and what it's consequences might be, we would slow fast.

Whatever was going on in his head, I could't stop what was going on in mine. Terror was creeping in. I felt intact, but my grip on composure was slipping. I knew his wound was bad. Gut wounds are nasty when they bleed out, but it's the lack of blood that alarmed me. No blood means something serious got hit. An organ. Something of meaning - an integral part of the machine, not just the joins. And the sight of the filth seeping into the inky chasm was squeezing my terror into a fever. We needed to get out.

We managed about 500 yards before the pace of the filthy river began to quicken, and I saw we were approaching a bowl where more similar sewer tunnels congregated on all sides. As if the smell could worsen, it somehow did. It burned the nostrils, and as I choked the taste back, my tainted spit burned my throat, and send the infernal flavor down my gullet. The risk of my own illness was heightening, but Steven's gunshot wound was so far beyond risk. I could picture infection gripping and ripping. I could see it. If not from the bullet presumably lodged somewhere within his person, then definitely from the shit swilling the wound.

The pace of the water was hastening further, at an alarming rate. I had tried body-boarding once on Anglesey, and that's the closest thing to the sensation I can describe. That suction of water around your midriff, the quiet pressure before the crash of foam. I looked ahead and saw that the bowl was deep and churning, waste frothing everywhere - and to the far right, a solitary broad exit pipe, 4 feet across. You couldn't see where it went, only that it was dark, and there was only a 6 inch or so clearance from the roof of the pipe to the surface just below it. To the far left of the bowl, the ledge a foot up leveled out into a proper platform about ten feet across - a viewing platform over which to check the workings of this massive overgrown toilet. It was also embedded into the tunnel walls, offering a bricked corner behind which to crouch. A vantage point, or hiding place, whichever - it was better than the uncertainty of the pipe opposite it. At the very least, it would give us the time to assess our next move - if indeed there would be one.

I motioned to Steven the ledge, and he gave me a nod of recognition. The colour was fast draining from him now but he did his best not to show what was going on. This, Kayla, is a fine example of your husband's bravery. Inside, his body must have been going into shutdown. But outside he was doing his best, probably trying to protect me, just like I had earlier tried to protect him. I waited for him, and we both approached the edge of the bowl, with caution. Falling would mean entering the bowl and whatever was in it. Looking at it and the spit and churn of the flow, I could't imagine what harmful debris was stuck in that bowl, never mind the current which would spit you out into that little pipe with barely any air. We edged, terrified for our footing, and saw there was five feet from the edge of the tunnel overspill to the brink of the platformed ledge - our sanctuary. Just before the edge of the bowl, there was a step up, as the waste spilled over into the bowl. I put my foot onto it, and threw myself at the ledge. With all my gear soaked, I was less than graceful in flight, but my hands felt dry concrete and I gripped for all I was worth. Purchase assured, I hoisted myself up, and reached immediately for Steven. His body was talking his mind out of the distance of the leap, and he looked shaky as he rose onto the step over the bowl. I reached out my rifle for him to grab, which he did. I knew the rifle could take the weight of a man, but I was less sure that either of our grips would hold. Steven swung out on the rifle like a vine, and was suddenly below me, dangling over the bowl. I pulled him up, and we were there - made it.

As I dragged him back into the recess of the platform, I almost forgot the smell, as we tasted this tiny victory. Just as we slumped down, I saw the fresh wet imprints of our bodies on the dry concrete, like alligator tracks in and out of a river. I hopped up immediately and tried to cover them with dust from the recess. Last thing we needed was discovery.

Satisfied, I turned back to Steven. But Steven didn't look great at all. The exertion looked like it had drained the last drops of fight from him. I took my gear off, and did the same for Steven. He winced a couple of times, and I asked him how his stomach was. And he responded with such grace that I almost did a double-take: 'Thank you'. That was all he said. I never asked him fully what he meant, and I'm not sure I care. At the time, I took at as 'You don't need to bullshit me, but you've been great so far'. I dropped the act, and told him what I thought about his wound, while getting him comfortable (well, as comfortable as possible on a ledge over a giant flushing toilet sodden with clothes covered in fetid human waste).

We lay there listening, trying to steady ourselves. Exertion leaves a footprint which eventually lifts, but Steven's exertion just wouldn't dissipate. The darkness wasn't complete, but my fears were now faultlessly constructed. I went through both of our packs. Some basic provisions, and a couple of containers of water - all covered in the sludge we pulled ourselves from. I used some water to clean Steven's wound as best I could, and a touch to rinse the provisions down, and to give our rifles a quick clean. We had 3 chocolate bars, a strawberry protein bar, two bags of crackers and some gummy bears. I broke open the first aid kit, rinsed that two, and found the little bottle of alcohol gel. I cleaned Steven up as best I could, but the dressings were all destroyed. All I could do was ration the water, ration the food, ration the alcohol gel, and hope for a solution. I didn't want to leave Steven to seek help - he wouldn't last. We could only rely on being discovered by the right people, but considering our radio's were destroyed, that looked bleak. Within the hour, a slow shock slipped over Steven, although his eyes remained focussed. He used his speech sparingly, and his body movements even more sparingly. And we sat there on that ledge for six days.

I won't go into detail about every day. I will regale what is important, but I can't dwell too hard here. I sat and cared for my best friend as best I could for 6 days, routinely cleaning and feeding him with what we had. What comes next will not be easy to read, and I picture it being as hard to digest as it is for me to write. As my pen hovers the page, I feel a phantom standing over me - a wrought twisted demon, bent by fury, that has had me at it's mercy every day since.

When we realized we weren't being pursued, I filled the air with quiet one-sided conversation. I told him not to talk. I talked for both of us. But by day 4, his pain really betrayed itself. He had been so stoic, so strong, staring a certain death in the face, but never admitting that it might get the better of him. He burst into a thick sob, that echoed off the bowl walls, and eventually got lost in the mulch. He told me he loved you. It was simple - the purity of it is as solid now as it was then. He loves you - now, then, forever. All time. He was yours. As he faced his death, it was you he was thinking about. People travel a lifetime not feeling that, and I am one of them. I now know that that sense of utter devotion and belonging that can only mean love is definite - love is REAL. My tears are hitting the page as I write this. I could only imagine feeling, just for a second, someone loving me the way he loved you. If you ever wonder how he felt about you, in the dark embrasures of your mind where concern festers, and time has blunted the truth of your love together, you now know. You were everything to him. And you were with him to the bitter end.

And then I get to your children. And I don't think I can write anymore. I watched him say his goodbye's to you all. Nothing I can write will justify what he said about the love he showed me for his family, but let me tell you, it was given away in the harsh painful sobbing in that dark sewer in Afghanistan. His anguish at never seeing you again, his torture at never telling you one more time he loved you - the hopelessness of knowing he would never be there to support you again, or to guide his children through the minefield of growing up... I have seen what it means to love, and it was simultaneously tragic and beautiful - the ultimate opera.

Which makes the next part all the harder to admit. The authorities know, and I would imagine you do too. There is a big DISHONORABLY DISCHARGED stamp next to my name for a reason, and that's the same reason I don't have a single medal to speak of.

On the evening of day 4, his sobbing subsided. Then he asked me to kill him. He told me the burning was too great inside, the ache in all parts of him too hard to bare anymore. Our fate looked sealed, with our rations wilting. I expected the sewer flow to abate at some point, to enable me to reconnoiter, but it never did. Forward progress was fantasy. He asked me time and again through the 5th day. I remained steadfast. He refused to beg, but he had a trump card. I had told him, during one of our many conversations on Bastion, I would do the exact same thing, and that I would expect any true friend to listen to my wishes. He had me trapped by my own reasoning and stubbornness, and he knew it. I could't argue with that. He told me that to kill him would be the greatest gift, to free him of the pain he was gripped by, to send him home to the heavens where he could watch over you and the kids. He said he had given everything for England, and there was nothing more to give. It was mission accomplished.

He begged all of day 5. There's nothing really knew to tell here, save for that it was perhaps the worst day of my life.

Eventually he went quiet at the start of the 6th day, and didn't speak again. His eyes were shut, and his breathing shallow. His energy reserves spent. After a breakfast of 1 inch of molded strawberry protein bar, I ended his life. It was instantaneous. I won't add anything else, but I did it with as much care and love as

I possibly could, which sounds just ludicrous. But it's true.

I was overcome. I was furious, devastated, confused, happy. All sorts of emotions that left me in a state of extreme emotional anxiety and delayed post traumatic stress, or so my discharge psychologists tell me. I stood, then hurled myself into the churning water of the bowl. I took nothing with me, rather let fate decide what should happen to this murderer. I remember the familiar tepid foul deluge, and falling into it. And I remember nothing else.

The next memory I have is a hospital bed back on Bastion. Confusion. Hate for myself. Hate for being alive, realizing that in survival, I would be forced to live with what I did. I was mocked by a higher power, forced to endure a punishment that to me, was worse than death. I had been prepared to meet my maker, but my maker wasn't ready for me - more than that he was intent on punishing me. And I would probably have done the same, if I was forced to decide the fate of someone who had done what I did.

As time passed, they told me what had happened. A fisherman had find me stuck against a grid at a river outlet, unconscious, pressed against the grating - 3 miles from the helicopter crash site. I was mangled from head to toe, but somehow carried the murmur of life. Which was enough for the fisherman to use me as a bargaining chip with my commanding officers. He originally wanted some munitions, but my superiors thought the munitions too valuable. They eventually bartered him down to some fast food from Bastion, which ironically wasn't all that far away. Literally, I was as valuable to my superiors as a Big Mac. If McDonald's need a hot new marketing hook, there you go. 'Big Mac - worth swapping a half dead soldier for'...

I lay in that bed for an awful 3 weeks, as a battle waged in and around me. Physically, I was strengthening, slowly but surely, but in contrast, my spirits were darkening. A gloom was setting in, and I near welcomed it. Hate became welcomed, and I gradually entrenched myself in a the dank mental tomb of depression. Since that very day, I have never once come out. I was gripped by a series of pretty nasty surface infections, but nothing too serious on the inside. Malnourishment was the main problem, and dehydration. The feverish side effects of both of these became the bricks and mortar for my depression. They constructed the walls in which I dwell in madness.

I eventually regained enough strength to answer all the questions I knew were coming, and at this point, a sub-plot began to emerge. I betrayed myself by giving in to the labels they wanted to assign me. What difference it would have made is anyone's guess, but... I told them I killed him. I confessed. I said I had to. They asked what alternatives I had, because, surely, given my survival, there was a way out. I didn't want to go through the long story of our hell on that ledge, fighting off every mental demon that may ever face you. They were right. There was a chance we both could have survived, if we both took our chances and dived into the cauldron. But neither of us did. And when they asked me this, I didn't fight it. I agreed that there was a chance. Such is my guilt, I agreed that there was a chance that things could have been different. I hung my head in shame, like a scolded dog. They may have guessed the truth but they didn't show it. They treated me like I was a man who had been given an opportunity, in an extreme setting, to take another man's life.

This is not a far-fetched scenario. Combat warps a man. The stress of war is just as bad. You are trained and trained, to the point of monotony, to kill. It becomes your be all and end all. There is nothing else but to kill. And in this mindset the act of killing is just as dangerous as not killing at all. To a less strong mind, killing can become a drug, the release of ending life an opiate beyond compare. The ultimate thrill in a setting where it is encouraged, and part of your job. Conversely, if you have not killed, but you have been expertly trained to kill, every moment up to that first kill is sparked with the crackle of intense anticipation. You know a kill is coming, you know that that most guttural and primitive of sensations will be activated, sooner or later. But what if it is never fulfilled? What then? I have heard of soldiers who go to great lengths to get that first kill out of the way, and to fulfill all that training. We are talking about an environment entirely preoccupied with the taking of life. The impact of this has many permutations, and releases many personalities. I mentioned earlier camp being like a huge psych ward - and thus we go full circle.

I was court marshaled. They painted me as a man who, in albeit an extreme circumstance, had killed a fellow soldier when survival alternatives were at hand. I was never accused of being an all-out murderer, but they stopped just short. Thanks to my service, they decided not to take it further than simply stripping me of my medals and dishonorably discharging me. Word was out that I had killed Steven, but somehow survived myself. That was enough for people to judge me. I sealed my decent into infamy by never setting anyone right. I was so awash with guilt, confusion. Steven had begged me to kill him. Just begged me. Just like I would have done if the roles were reversed.

I was shipped back to England, the previous 9 years of my life wiped from the slate. I came back with no record, no history, no nothing. I didn't have a place, a purpose or a home - especially after my parents took umbrage with my decision in the sewer. I hoped that they would see my rationale, at least understand my position and why I did what I did. But no such luck. I was home for an extremely uncomfortable 2 days, and, even though they never kicked me out, I took the initiative and left. Their son had gone from hero to zero in the blink of an eye, and their own pride took a massive hit in the balls. I think they were scared of the questions and the ensuing scrutiny, so I left. Neither party has contacted the other since that day. I was left with the money I had earned through my years of service, which had been steadily dripped into my home account from overseas. I had no dependents, and no plans for the money, so it was all still there. We are not talking about a great amount of cash, but enough to keep me afloat as I work out what to do next.

But at present, I can't do anything next. You see, I'm banged up in prison, on a murder charge that I can't shake. Some would say it's justice. I'm inclined to agree with them. I've made some poor choices in my life, and I keep making them. But I'm in a spiral that won't relent, and I chase violence for a purpose I am yet to comprehend. I had become nothing more than a brutal problem-solver, not by design but by accident. And I got a taste for it, and it put me behind bars.

There is a paradox at work. I don't recognize anything anymore. This place is not the same to me. I don't see England as my own. I don't even see it as England. England is an ideal and nothing more. I can't believe I gave up everything to protect this morass I don't even recognize anymore. But I will never give up on what England means to me. I can sense a fight in me. I can feel my rebellion boiling. If I get the chance I will do what I can to keep my England safe - even though my England hates me and wants to bury me as deep as it can dig. And I do it with the memory of Steven as my mascot.

If I ever do anything worthwhile with my life, I do it in the spirit of Steven's memory. The courage he showed, I will too. The spirit he exhibited, I'll do the same. The unrelenting good... I can't give that. I'm not 'good'. The 'good' I had died with him. But I will work for the cause of 'good', and hope that that will be good enough.

Kayla, I leave you to your own conclusions. What I wanted to do was set the record straight so that you know what really happened, and so that I know you found out just how much Steven loved you. I need you to know that. I can't carry it around anymore without you knowing it.

I also want you to know I am sorry. I did what I did out of love and respect. Don't you dare forgive me. I won't ever forgive myself either.

All the best in life, and know that once upon a time, you were loved very much.

Ben"

3

Dag's eyes lift from the page, and drift out onto the prison. It looks just the same as it did moments before. Yet, inside there is a man festering and bubbling over, a man so in need of help yet too hurt to ever accept it. Dag feels for him, and acknowledges again the similarities he felt with him when he first met Ben on that peculiar and demonic night in North Wales, when Dag had saved Ben's life from an indoctrinated spiritual congregation.

Dag always thought there were dark events that led Ben to where he finds himself, and in a sense, he was right - only he was not expecting the story to be quite so sad, and painful, and perhaps, for it to resonate so forcefully with Dag. He too had had difficult decisions to make in combat, but nothing like the choices Ben faced. It is deeply sobering, and before Dag knows what has happened, he has been sitting in his car for 15 minutes in silence, just thinking.

He folds the letter, and put it back in the envelope. The seal is ripped, but he knows he can just get a new envelope and copy the address from the old envelope to the new one. More bothering to him, was whether he should send it at all.

This Kayla, wherever she may be, may have put these demons to bed a long time ago. She may have moved on, she may have a new life. She may know the circumstances of her husbands death in far more gruesome detail than Ben has been able to divulge. She may be happy. Or as happy as can be expected.

Is it right to give this letter to her? Would it bring up things that just shouldn't be brought up? If the letter doesn't make it, Ben would never know the difference. He openly guarantees he won't contact her, so it's not like he'll ever see Kayla to confirm it's receipt. Ben's darkness is so complete, his mindset so carefully arranged in such absolute terms, that Dag is unsure whether anyone else should be burdened by it's weight.

Dag sits there, clogged by indecision. He feels as if he might sit there forever, just staring at the prison walls, digesting what he has read and hoping that the passage of time will allow it to help him make a decision. But he can't bring himself to move. He just sits there holding the letter.

It is dark before he turns on the car engine, his decision made. He just hopes it is the right one - and in truth, he knows he will never know the answer to that. He drives off, leaving the sprawling urban prison behind him, and the tortured soul it conceals firmly encased inside, toiling and troubled, waiting for a chance at something resembling redemption.

FROM STEEL

1

It is a horrible sound. That repetitive scrape of plastic against concrete. Over and over again, a solitary fingernail across an infinite blackboard. It has been this way for well over two hours now, but the man who is creating the sound seems as devoted as ever, and shows no sign of abating.

Ben Bracken lies in his bunk, completely swallowed by the infernal sound, but doesn't cover his ears. He listens to the sound, it's repetition, and tries to find comfort in it's routine. He can't at all, because he knows what it is for. He rolls onto his side, the small bed creaking as he shifts, and he looks to the floor.

A man is crouched by the corner of the small cell, reaching behind the toilet bowl to hide his actions. Ben knows what he is doing - using the concrete walls of the cell to sharpen the handle of a toothbrush into an ugly point. The main hides the scrape marks behind the toilet in an attempt to cover his tracks - so that when this hasty shank is found on the floor by someone bleeding to death, it will not so easily lead back to this very cell.

The man checks the progress of the sharpening handle, and seems pleased. He smiles grimly.

'Should be good for two or three hits, then will probably break off in the bugger. Perfect.' he says.

Ben frowns, and then rolls away again, trying to achieve a little rest and calm before the inevitable frantic scenes that will ensue from his cellmate's preparations.

As Ben turns to face the wall, and the incessant scratch resumes, he sighs. 20 months. That's how long he has been there, give or take. He doesn't know exactly in days. When he was locked up for 17 years with no eligibility for appeal until 15 years in, bothering about counting days seems a little hopeful and futile to Ben. He didn't bother.

He is in Strangeways Prison, Manchester - a mammoth brick hulk cripplingly close to the city centre, but far away enough to remind you that you are no longer part of it. He has been in the same cell all that time, but his cellmate has changed twice. This most recent addition, a local Salford lad doing time for GBH and armed robbery, has been with him 3 weeks, and has scrapped and fought every second of that. He goes by the name of Craggs, and admits his crimes in full - but that doesn't stop him from believing he shouldn't be there. He is, Ben firmly asserts, a vicious little twerp lost in a gangster lifestyle he has adopted from rap videos.

Ben told him this when he arrived, having kicked off about preferring Ben's bunk, and threatened to have Ben killed by his 'mans on the outside, gats blazing'. Ben almost broke down in laughter at hearing that, and reminded Craggs that they aren't in Compton, and that Ben himself is doing 17 years for murder. Craggs nearly pissed his pants on hearing that, but within a couple of days, he was telling all and sundry how he himself was so 'hard' that they had him holed up with the cold killers. Ben didn't like being spoken of in such a way, but if it gave him a quiet life, he would reluctantly take it.

And now Craggs has a beef with someone elsewhere in this hell-hole, and is fashioning an ugly looking weapon to settle things. Ben can't help thinking how pathetic it is - how this man chases a life of uncertainty and violence, lost in the perceived glamour of it all. Is it England's fault for not giving him anything to identify with, or is it MTV for giving him something so over-stylized to latch on to? Who knows, thinks Ben, acknowledging, that really he couldn't give a shit. Another symptom, that's all. Besides, Ben has bigger fish to fry.

The last 20 months have been fantastic for Ben, despite obviously being behind bars. Like the toothbrush-dagger, only much less hastily prepared, he too has sharpened in prison. He has cleared his mind, and brushed away the muddled cobwebs of confusion, doubt and self-loathing that dogged him before - not least thanks to the letter he sent to Steven's wife Kayla. After all this time, setting the record straight felt very good indeed, and has allowed him a new lease of life (well, within the confines of the prison routine). He has diligently kept to a gym routine that has seen his body strengthen also - and of course, he hasn't touched a drop of alcohol since he crossed the prison threshold. He feels 10 stories tall.

Ben has also, finally, assigned himself a purpose. Society seemed reluctant to give him one, the events prior to his incarceration assigned him one, but now? He has something to believe in, something to fight for. And he is convinced he will get his chance soon.

He has no respect at all for the people or circumstances that placed him there, but he does still believe in good. Remembering Steven taught him that. He firmly believes good exists but it is so rare and hidden at times, and it must be cherished and protected - just like any beautiful, endangered species in the animal kingdom.

Also, like the animal kingdom, he has decided, within reason, to apply his own law. This is borne out of his complete lack of faith in the execution of laws today. The pliability of law is something that always bothered him, the varieties of it's interpretation unsettling, allowing the wrong-doers leeway via red-tape and bureaucracy. Ben has decided that where good is concerned, he will be it's judge. And he will decide what happens next with a clear conscious. He intends to right wrongs as and when the occasions provide. He has no interest in looking for trouble, but he is well aware that trouble cannot be ignored. He also has no penchant for seeking violence, but he knows in this area, he is proficient. And if violence can be used in the protection of such wrongs? Ben will damn well commit it.

The problem for Ben, is his predicament. In prison, his ability to protect good is somewhat limited, granted. But he does not agree at all with being there.

The trial itself was as quick and brutal as the death of Markland Masters, which had seen Ben arrested. Factor into that the death of Keith Sinfield in Manchester (who Ben certainly did kill, throwing him out of Beetham Tower to rain down onto Deansgate), and a Molly Cleverson in Llanberris (who he threw on a bonfire) and a pretty damning picture emerges. But the only charges that they could completely pin on Ben were relating to Markland's death, as he was caught in the act. Ben's involvement in the other deaths was acknowledged by almost all, but there was no evidence. Ben's defense lawyer, Mr Selwyn Barraclough, had rightly pointed out there was not a shred of evidence to prove he had done any of those things, never mind the one that he actually didn't do, which was Markland.

Nevertheless, by this point Ben had quickly accepted that his lack of trust and faith in the justice system was chronic and permanent, and suggested he would plead guilty to the one charge and get a lesser sentence - rather than fight all 3 charges, lose the case and be faced with a life sentence - or multiple life sentences, if they drudged up too much of his past and had to factor in Steven's death in that Afghan sewer all those years ago.

The prosecution quickly accepted, seeing another win tucked swiftly under it's belt - justice prevails again. Ben again feeling the pointed end of a compromised society's morality stick. At that point, Ben just wanted to escape it all, feeling disillusioned with the England he had come back to and foolish for the haphazard nature of his arrest. Plus, frankly, he felt he deserved punishment. And away he went.

Craggs interrupts Ben's thoughts. 'I think it's ready. Just in time for rec hour'.

Now, Ben's mind - piqued and lucid from his time off - is ready, and his body readier. He has a plan to get out. It's almost time to put it into action - and recreation hour is where it all starts.

2

A bleak, droning buzzer emanates for somewhere in the bowels of the prison, echoing through the halls and permeating Ben and Craggs' cell. Craggs almost leaps out of his skin at the sound, while Ben merely sits up. Off to the main mess hall, to watch the pointless prison ecosystem at work. There is an obvious hierarchy, a nasty order of life in this prison, where those entrusted with upholding the law are as serpentine as those they are paid to keep in line. Ben has no respect for the prison, nor the people that run it - he has seen so much corruption in here, that every drop of faith he had was slowly squeezed away. He doesn't believe in this place, and conversely, he gets the feeling this place doesn't believe in him either. All Ben's rehabilitation (if that's what you can call it) was undertaken by himself. Ben has tried to be a model prisoner at times, if only to keep his nose out of trouble - never because he was encouraged.

Craggs is at the door, toothbrush shank in hand, waiting for the door to be opened. Usually takes within 2 minutes for the door to be unlocked remotely, and then they are ushered down to the main mess hall, by two guards. Ben and Craggs, despite their violent pasts, are not classed as violent risks - there are others in the prison of far higher priority in those terms and budget cuts and austerity measures had seen Ben and Craggs fall down the pecking order in terms of priority. This pleases Ben no end, as far as his plan is concerned. The doors open with an earthy crunch, and Craggs steps forward.

'Conceal it, for crying out loud', spits Ben. Despite himself, Ben finds himself having to instruct Craggs - after all, if Craggs marches out of here weapon in hand, it makes both of them look bad. And Ben is hoping that today, like all days, his own behaviour will be looked on favourably. Well, especially today.

As the door opens, and the familiar harsh smell of industrial cleaning products fills the men's noses and scratches the back of their throats, Ben hops up and follows Craggs into the hallway - and while doing so he shoves the makeshift shank up his sleeve. They turn left, and immediately walk directly up the dark hallway, where two burly wardens wait for them. Ben knows them both, but he knows that they rotate. Today is Thursday, and Thursday means they get the pleasure of Ronson and Dunn to escort them through the prison. They beckon them forward with batons. Craggs walks with not so much a spring in his step but an entire pilled-up jack-in-a-box, energy rippling out of every pore. Ben ribs him.

'Keep cool,' Ben whispers.

'I can't, I'm fucking jacked' Craggs replies. Ben knows this could mean either he is less inclined to bottle it, and will go for it all in, or he may, in a jittery fit, botch the whole thing. Either way, it's too late for team talks. Ben is still confident that his plan is solid, but he needs Craggs to play his part - and what a part it is.

'Come on you two' bellows Dunn. 'Queer-baits this way'. Ben can't really disguise his dislike for these two, but he knows just how pathetic they are, and how little they are worth his time. Getting one over these two is not key to his plan, but a happy side-effect if all comes off well. They are two who would just as easily be on Ben's side of the iron bars, if it weren't for their position here in Strangeways. Their behaviour in here alone should have seen them charged and imprisoned long ago, but the fact that they are not only proves Ben's assertions and strengthens his resolve to beat this godforsaken system.

As they walk past the two guards, Ronson slaps Ben's arse. Ben froths at the affront, but only inwardly. It only makes Ben hope he sees these two twits' faces with figurative egg all over them later, when they witness what he has done and what it means for them.

Ben also knows that the sexual element of the banter is only to exert power over them, as they test how far they can take the exercising of their power. It's designed to objectify and put them down, much like archaic societies would do to their women. Reduce individuality and personality from them, and sabotage their footing so that they can never gain proper societal hold. And it only makes Ben pity them more.

Over his period of incarceration, he has seen many different examples of the staff's abuse of their position, ranging from the minute (kind of like what Ben just experienced) and the pretty grand (beatings, framings, you name it - anything to keep the power where it is). It took Ben about 2 minutes to realize he didn't care about this at all - to care would only dilute his resolve to leave this place, and leave he must. So he never argued with the injustice, never took umbrage when the staff's whims affected his own comfort and wellbeing. He just kept his head down, waited and planned - simmering.

Ben has become all too used to sorting out problems with violence - so much so that when he decided that he was going to do something about his predicament, he was faced with the stumbling block of acknowledgement that, on this occasion, if he really wanted out of here, he was going to have to do so with cold intelligence and foresight. Ben found the process of doing so extremely informative and liberating, and has concocted a plan that - now the wheels are in motion - would have hopefully two very possible outcomes. Namely that it would both see Ben offered the door to freedom with no questions asked and a slap on the back, and would see the entire prison rocked to its corrupt foundations and instigate real fundamental change in its governance. Either way, Ben is happy that the wind is going to change one way or the other - and only for the better where his well-being is concerned.

He just needs to keep an eye on Craggs, who is marching next to Ben a little too quickly.

'You look like a man who has got some serious business to attend to' whispers Ben. 'If you want to get this done, you have to keep cooler than this.'

'What's it matter to you?' Craggs fires back.

'You are not going to get close to him at this rate, you'll end up back in the cell with me and I'll have to listen to you pissing and moaning every night while you work out how you screwed your chance up. Keep it together and you'll have your shot.'

Craggs reluctantly slows a touch, and drops into the same stride pattern as Ben. To be associated with a deluded scumbag like Craggs would ordinarily bother Ben greatly, but today, if he has to take Craggs by the hand, he'll damn well do it. They approach the central mess facility, it's hulking blue safety door manned by another warden.

The door is opened for them, and the dense din of the prison ecology wafts out immediately, an airborne audio mulch that clangs towards the approaching men. They cross through the doorway, and survey the scene. About 35 inmates sit dotted across 10 rows of tables, little groups of men already formed rows apart. Recreation time is staggered to allow for smaller groups of 30-40 inmates to circulate, with a different mix everyday. Ben thinks it is actually quite sensible - it's theory is to stop resentment boiling and frictions emerging. It would work perfectly, if it weren't for the fact that the staff are too wrapped up in their own thing, drunk on their own power, to really commit to the planning of a system that would appear unpredictable to the inmates. Everyone has worked it out long before today. Factions have emerged and bonded, and they know what days and sessions they will see each other again. It's become as organized and as routine-friendly as weekly village book club get togethers.

But it has all helped in Ben's planning. He had committed to memory this routine, which allowed for him to plan so carefully. It allows him to do little things like exactly that which he is doing right now, as he walks through the door - he glances over to the right far wall, where the quiet bleeders and readers sit. They are named as such thanks to the similarities between two groups: those that sit quietly and hope that the prison experience passes them by without too much incident and horror, and those that adopt a fashion just as quiet, but sneak along using anything and everything they can to swim along easier. They latch themselves on to all the other groups in the prison, like a parasitic barnacle on the belly of much bigger sea dwellers, trying to eke what they can from the relationship. It hacks off most, and they are more often kicked back. The readers never protest, so the bleeders use them as a hub. Just another example of inner-prison politics.

Maddock is a bleeder, and was very happy to make the acquaintance of Ben, the enigmatic soldier turned murderer. Ben encouraged their contact for one solitary purpose - for his ability to do something special. Maddock, behind the scenes, could get things in and out of the prison, with particular success at the latter. And if Ben is to succeed today, he needs to get something out. He dropped the package with Maddock two days previously, in another supposed random cobbling together of inmates in the prison gym. Ben took an extra large wash-bag to the weight-room that day. The deal to process the bag out had already been sealed, thanks to Ben's negotiation powers regarding prison commodities. Certain things are currency inside the walls, where money still has power but not as much power as cigarettes, sex or food. Ben didn't have any of the first two to give up, but thanks to Ben's various volunteering jobs around the prison, viable to him thanks to his spotless behavior, he did have some rather sought-after Green and Black's Dark Chocolate that had been found in a handbag left in the 'lost and found' bin after someone's conjugal visit. It seems the present was forgotten about, more pressing matters at hand. As Ben glances over to the group, as he and Craggs head to the coffee dispensers stationed on the far wall, Maddock catches Ben's eye and nods cheerfully - and Ben now knows the bag, and it's vital contents, are out of the prison away to somewhere they can really mean something.

The bag's displacement from prison doesn't mean that they can't turn back now, but it does mean that if Craggs does what he so incessantly asserts he can and will, Ben's plan is well in it's way to a successful outcome. But the very placement of Craggs deed is very important, as is who and what witnesses it. Namely, the cameras.

Ben pours himself a coffee, deliberately not offering one to Craggs, who still sticks by his side. Ben is reluctant to give caffeine to Craggs, and jitter the jitters further. Showing a wherewithal Ben didn't expect, Craggs senses this, and turns to face the various groups in the room. Ben pours the coffee, hoping it's caffeine kick will be the one last twist of the pencil sharpener before the big exam, sending him into the oncoming events in the best possible fashion. Ben feels ready, no doubt, and as he sips the ascetic sludge he glances skywards - to give the cctv one last check over.

The room is covered by three cameras, wide over each of the three entrances to the room. Ben had guessed largely at the viewing angle covered by each unit, and had worked out one pocket of dead space lodged in the back right corner of the room - directly under one camera, just out of the gaze of the other two. Austerity measures again, thinks Ben - the prison's enforced cheapness giving jigsaw pieces for his plan. He unhurriedly gravitates them both into the hidden corner, and leans against the wall, facing the hall.

'It has to be in this corner,' says Ben quietly to Craggs. 'Like we discussed.'

'I'm not a dummy,' Craggs responds sulkily.

'Then no excuses for fucking up' Ben hits back. 'Is he here yet?'

'Not yet.'

'Keep an eye out.'

Craggs fidgets, rubbing his eye nervously. Ben worries he might take his own eye out with the secret shank if he's not careful, which would certainly put the mockers on things.

Ben too is waiting for someone to arrive, and he scans the rafters diligently. It's a figure he sees every day, and who's impact is always felt. It's someone he has spoken to on only a handful of incidents, but who always leaves an impression. It's an impression of irrepressible smugness, sheer intoxication of his standing and rancid arrogance. A fat man, who always seems levered into suits too small, making it look like he is much more overweight that he actually is - Harry Tawtridge, Chief Warden. He is a man that Ben has seen abuse his position more than anybody else in

Strangeways, on each conceivable level. He has stolen money and possessions from inmates, instigated beatings on which to gamble among the guards, paid for silence when things have gotten beyond him, dished out punishments with scant regard for rhyme, reason or consistency. Ben has always despised the actual physical things Tawtridge has done, but it's his overall personality and attitude which Ben finds deplorable and serves to crystallize how repugnant he is. He once told an inmate that he looks forward to his family visiting so he can get a look at the inmate's 14 year old daughter, who he described as 'ripening'. He made an inmate dance a striptease on a dining table for vital asthma medication. It turns Ben's stomach.

Tawtridge dwells on the rafters above, on a high platform overlooking his kingdom, while the guards stand on a gangway lower, keeping eager watch.

'He's here' whispers Craggs, breaking Ben's train of thought. Ben tries not to take too much notice, but he needs to get a fix on Quince - the hapless bastard who's day will come to an abrupt end.

3

Through the same door that Ben and Craggs had arrived, saunters a man so average he almost fades into ignominy as he walks. He arrives with little physical fanfare, and his appearance matches perfectly the lack of fireworks. Short hair, clean shaven, not ugly but not a dish, just... nondescript. He could be a pedestrian in Grand Theft Auto - there to flesh out the background, to add depth to the scene, but ultimately pointless. And exactly like in GTA, immediately susceptible to a sticky end.

Ben feels that Craggs has stiffened next to him, coiled tight with the morbid electricity of the deed that is to come.

'Take a breath,' Ben whispers. 'Keep lucid'.

'Don't tell me to keep lucid. I'm gonna slice this prick.'

'We need to wait. Beckon him over in a moment, get him in position. You'll know when it's time.'

'Why can't I just stick him now?'

Ben had his own reasons why that couldn't be the case, but to divulge them would let too much of the cat out of the bag and strip Craggs of his big moment - because it will also be Ben's big chance, if it goes right. Civility is also important - they need to make it look like everyone is on good terms until the deed itself.

'Because,' Ben explains, 'you need to get away with it, don't you. I don't care what a murder charge would do to your street cred, but you need to give the powers that be a fragment of doubt. That starts with the guards not seeing it, and the videos missing it.'

Craggs thinks about this for a moment, the gears near-visibly whirring. 'Yeah', he simply says. His right hand stays wedged firmly into his pocket. Good, thinks Ben - he can now focus on the next part of his plan, so he walks into the main body of the room and takes a seat at an empty table. Once there he looks over at Quince, just as a flicker of light high in his peripheral vision makes him look skywards. Silhouetted by a garish halogen bulb, a round and angular shape that can only be attributed to a large man in a suit. Tawtridge.

No time like the present. Immediately, Ben strokes his chin - the signal to Craggs that it's OK to proceed.

Craggs takes a deep breath, and waves animatedly in Quince's direction. This does precisely nothing, and Quince keeps perusing for a seat.

Craggs lifts his fingers to his mouth, and whistles loudly. This causes a few heads to turn, and the volume in the room to dip a touch. Quince himself looks over, finally, to which Craggs makes a beckoning gesture with his hand.

Quince looks surprised, as if to say 'me?' and Craggs gives him an easy thumbs up - what could possibly go wrong? Ben is mentally checking off the progress, and everything is ticked off so far.

Quince makes his way through the throng, leaving a small wave of faces turning to the corner. Last thing for Ben to check is another plant in the crowd - so he glances 10 feet from the corner, at the nearest reinforced door to the hall. It's clear, as it should be, and sitting at the nearest inconspicuous seat, staring at Ben with simmering intent, is the big, round, eager face of Hopkins. Hopkins has been there 4 years, and it's been four years too many - and everyone knows it. It is the single worst kept secret inside the prison walls. He tells everyone his desire to escape, wardens, inmates, cooks, cleaners, whoever. He's still got 7 to go. He is in Ben's eyes, simply put, just too dense to attempt anything - like so many, all mouth, no trousers.

So, on this occasion, Ben has given him the trousers if he has the balls to wear them. He whispered it to him in the lunch line on Tuesday just gone. For a couple of seconds, on Thursday's afternoon rec room session, the door by the back left corner will be open for a couple of seconds. If he wants to have a go at getting out, he'll never have a better opportunity. He just has to man up and take it. And here he is, sitting like a loyal bloodhound waiting to fulfill his destiny. Ben nods so slightly to him that it barely appears as a movement - more of a ghost of a nod. Hopkins reads it loud and clear, and waits.

Quince gets nearer, only fifteen feet now.

Ben knows it is go time. All the pieces are in place. As Quince arrives in the corner, Ben faces the people who are still watching the corner. Out of nowhere, almost surprising to Ben despite his knowledge of Craggs' intentions, the quiet is punctuated by a series of thuds, the shriek of a stricken man, and the faces in front of him turning to grim surprise. He assumes that Craggs has done what he asserted so many times he would, and the next thing he sees is Craggs himself walking calmly across the room, back in full view.

The bare horror of this brutal moment, stripped of the usual uproar of a sudden violent attack, shocks Ben - the sheer blunt ugliness of it. For the first time, Ben feels guilty.

A moment passes of crystal near-silence. Nobody moves. Nobody dares breathe. All that can be heard is the soft footsteps of Craggs walking across the middle of the floor, and the odd scrape and rustle coming from Quince's direction. The fact that Quince is not making any vocal sounds suggests to Ben that Craggs must have got him pretty good. The snapshot of time seems to last forever as Ben waits...

And then it happens. A loud siren echoes from what sounds like deep in the earth below the prison, like the distant alarm over London during the Blitz. Then follows shouting from above.

'Nobody move!' a guard shouts, but Ben can't see where it came from. He looks up, to try to get a fix on Tawtridge, but now he can't see him in the lofty shadows. 'Everybody stay where you are!' another voice bellows.

The quiet returns, and everyone sits stock still. Quince has stopped scratching about in the corner, and Craggs has found a seat, both hands on the table in front of him, a crooked, smug smile on his face below narrowed eyes. Ben feels like shaking his head at the sight of that, and can only look at him as a poor deluded misguided little shit. Then Ben remembers that he must take responsibility for some of the misguidance, so he backs off on the thought a touch.

The door by the corner bursts open, and guards storm in. The first four run to the grounded Quince, and more pour in. Hopkins glances at Ben, in urgent need of approval, and Ben gives him one last push with a nod. Three more guards enter, making a grand total of six inside the rec room, and as the door is swinging shut behind what seems to be the last guard to enter the scene, Hopkins leaps to his feet and barrels at the door as fast as he can.

He makes it, just, and is into the corridor beyond. And this sparks utter pandemonium.

A second inmate, in seeing someone make a break for it, can't resist temptation, and makes a break for it also. Human nature takes over, that fear of being left out, and that, combined with the exposed opportunity to attempt escape through a quickly closing door, proves to much for others, and the door is bombarded with almost ten other inmates who follow.

The guards leap into action, swinging with batons - forgetting Quince, who is well into shock and on his way to death. The batons connect with prisoners, as the guards try to keep the inmates back from the door, but they can't stop an initial wave of perhaps four getting through. More and more prisoners are on their feet now, enraged by the sight of their fellow inmates copping a beating.

So far, so good for Ben, as a violent melee breaks out, and the situation is quickly ascending into an all out riot. Ben remains seated, as chairs squeak all around him as more and more prisoners get to their feet, and the skirmish between guards and inmates escalates with every shout and every crunching baton blow.

Ben waits, but he can't wait long - more guards are surely en route. He watches the door, and bides his time, the commotion gathering, punches flying, fifteen inmates against six guards... when Ben spots his opening. The door is open, wide and clear. He sprints for his own freedom.

4

Ben runs, dodging deftly two other prisoners who head for the fray, and others that had the same idea as him. As Ben gets to the door, he is one of three who get there at the same time, and he is jostling for position with two other blokes eager for that taste of freedom. In front is a stairwell landing, with two options - go up or down.

'Down is out guys', says Ben, 'Go for it'. Without hesitation, they do. Ben gives them a split second to make a start, then he jogs up the flight of stairs, completely opposite to his fellow escapees. He ascends one floor, then two, then three. He pauses, to catch his breath for a second, then approaches the door at the right of this elevated landing. Through the window and the wire grating of the door, he can see Tawtridge standing high on a gantry surrounded by lights, overlooking the rec hall. He has one hand on his head, the other in his mouth chewing his nails. His body on edge like a cat, he looks down anxiously.

Ben knows that the door should be locked, and he tries it anyway - and to his damn-near joy, he finds it open. Tawtridge's feeling of invincibility has led him down a dangerously lazy path, and Ben feels Tawtridge is extremely lucky that it is Ben himself who has found him and nobody else. He opens the door, and at once the sound of the cavernous space above the riot fills his ears. Yelping, clattering, shattering, clamouring. The sound of brutality and flight. Above the commotion, Tawtridge doesn't hear Ben's arrival.

'Chief Warden' shouts Ben.

Tawtridge spins around, sweat flicking from his face as he moves. He looks like hell - a picture definition of the 'stuck pig' metaphor, if ever there was one. He looks scared by Ben's presence, as if his moment has finally come.

'It's OK, Chief Warden,' Ben soothes but with urgency, 'But we need to go now.'

Tawtridge stands and processes this. Distrust oozes from him, and wrought indecision.

'I'm not here for trouble - I'm here to do my time, better myself and go home. And I feel that getting you to safety is the right thing to do.'

No movement from Tawtridge, but glass shattering from below punctures and clatters up to them.

'I am a soldier. You know this about me. I am bound by a sense of duty, it's what got me here in the first place. Duty says I need to get my commanding officer to safety, and in this scenario, that's you. But we need to go now.'

That works - Tawtridge is moving to Ben, a shuffle at first but then quicker steps. In a moment, they are back in the stairwell.

'Your office is reinforced? With a panic button?' Ben asks.

'Yes' replies Tawtridge.

'We need the quickest way there that does not go down. I don't want anyone to see you.'

'We need to go, up... and across, over the rec hall.' Tawtridge stutters and fumbles his words weakly.

'Then lead the way. I'll get you there. And run.'

And with that, they run up the next flight of stairs, clanging as they go. Ben glances down the gap through the middle of the stairwell, and sees hands grasping the bannister as they rise.

'They are coming Chief Warden. Keep moving.'

At the next metal landing, there are a number of openings, down which one could travel, but the central opening straight ahead is the widest, and it is the one that Tawtridge heads for. Behind Ben, there is a the familiar steel-tinged thudding of footsteps on the stairs below, echoing up the spine of the stairwell. This could well put things in jeopardy if they are sighted.

'Faster' he commands.

Tawtridge ups from nervous jog to an all out free-wheeling sprint. Ben keeps pace with him, while glancing back often at the increasingly smaller entrance at the far end of the corridor. Nothing there yet, but it can't be long.

'How far?' he asks.

'We are... over... the rec room... On... the other side... down two flights...', Tawtridge manages through ragged breaths.

Ben can see they are getting closer to another opening. He just hopes that on their travels they don't stumble into any fleeing prisoners who have managed to get lost on their search for an outlet to Manchester. God knows the tumult they are running directly above, and what has become of Quince and Craggs.

Mercifully the corridor ends and opens into another metal landing, with stairs on the immediate left. Tawtridge almost tumbles down the stairs, such is the abandon he throws himself at them with. He regains his footing and presses on. Ben follows, but as he does, he acknowledges that the footsteps behind now carry a duller, quieter echo - those following are in the corridor, gaining on them. Whether the pursuers know who it is they are following is unknown to Ben, but he doesn't care - avoiding them is key, and if they see Tawtridge, they will surely rip him limb from limb. And Ben needs him alive.

After descending two stories, Tawtridge exits onto the landing and pushes straight through one of two metal doors - again unlocked. As they do so, they hear the immediate clanging of footsteps traveling the stairs from whence they just came. Their pursuers are gaining. They enter a corridor that is markedly different to the others they have travelled down, the walls no longer dark grey unfinished breeze blocks, but now more of a finished gloss magnolia. Brighter, for another purpose.

After 25 yards, a door appears on the left wall. Tawtridge jangles his keys out of his pocket.

'Shit... Shit...' he says, as he frantically selects the right key from a thick wad and opens the door. Ben clocks the selfishness and carelessness of leaving a number of doors unlocked through laziness, and Tawtridge keeping his own little sanctuary bubble-wrapped. They enter into the office, just as on the landing behind them, through the glass on the door, Ben catches a blurred glimpse of two men in prison issues hit the landing. He doesn't wait to be noticed, and follows Tawtridge into the office, hoping to God that the men didn't notice, but fully expecting that they may well have.

5

The office is stuffy, with a coppery airborne hint of mold. Tawtridge locks the door behind them, and makes sure the blind on the door viewing glass is tightly shut. Ben surveys the room, and waits, marveling at the full bin, the cluttered desk, the papers piled on the floor, the picture of Tawtridge himself with two laughing boys and a collie. A different side to the man. Much less glamorous. Ben didn't know what he expected, but it wasn't this. Maybe a bank of flat-screens with cctv feeds, elaborate security shutters, a side table with a whiskey decanter on it... He is surprised at this reveal of near-budget-less middle management.

Quiet pervades. The men seemingly haven't pursued - at least for now.

Tawtridge gasps air, his mouth still lunging for it and grasping. After a moment, his breathing slows and he turns to Ben.

'Bracken, don't think for one minute that getting me out of there is going to get you any kind of special treatment. You're still just a face wandering faceless halls.'

Ben almost smiles here, especially now he knows its time for his own big reveal.

'I'm not expecting any special treatment at all. What I demand goes a bit beyond 'special treatment',' Ben counters.

'What the fuck are you on about?', Tawtridge rises to full height, spreading his mass, like like a fat featherless peacock in a suit.

'We both know you're not going out there again while all that is going on, so you're going to have to hear me out,' Ben says, as he perches on the edge of Tawtridge's desk. The mere action of infringing on Tawtridge's property like this both excites Ben and riles Tawtridge himself. 'Besides, I think you'll find it quite important.'

Tawtridge softens a touch, as if he knows his conduct may finally have caught up with him.

Ben continues. 'Let's see how much attention the shepherd pays to his flock.'

'If that is in reference to me, I know everything that goes on around here. Everything.'

'Then you'll know what volunteer jobs I do.'

'I know you like to portray yourself as a good little worker, a right busy little bee, eager to please - as if doing a few odd jobs is going to put a dent in your sentence, you idiot. We all know you're here for the duration.'

'What jobs exactly?'

'Laundry detail, primarily. But I know you offered to help on the blood donation day last week, among other things.'

'You've got it in one.'

'What's that got to do with anything?'

'Well, it would explain how a handful of warden uniforms went missing last week, doesn't it?'

Tawtridge takes that in for a second, but bristles again.

'Prisoners clothing is washed in a separate session to uniforms, you know that.'

Ben can only smile at that. 'You believe that? I put it you that you are so preoccupied with your gratuitous little power-trip around this place that you over-look finer detail. Rather, actually, that you assume the final detail is taken care of. Are there, or are there not, 5 guard uniforms missing?'

Tawtridge doesn't answer but words are unnecessary in answering. His eyes scream the affirmative, and his jowls wobble with anger.

'Now, you mentioned another of my other little do-gooder jobs. The blood drive,' Ben says, folding his arms across his chest with more than a hint of smugness. He has been waiting for this moment a while

- it is a moment he imagines any man who has served time under Tawtridge's bent governance would appreciate - and he wants to savour it. 'What if... In helping with converting the room back from a blood donation clinic to a simple snooker room, some... blood went missing.'

'Woop-di-do' Tawtridge taunts. 'You've got some prisoner's blood. Fantastic. What's your point?'

'Are you not interested to hear who's blood I have? Or, I should say, *had*?'

'I don't care. I literally couldn't care less. What difference does it make?'

'Who's the kid who got knifed today?'

Tawtridge stumbles for the words, crawling across the broken shards of his brain to try to find the right name. Ben puts him out of his misery.

'Quince,' Ben says. 'Richard Quincey'.

Tawtridge meets Ben's eyes. 'That's him.'

'Nasty way to go,' says Ben, grimly. 'I'd feel bad if he wasn't just another underbelly-feeding gutter-worm. Someone had to be the fall-guy. There wasn't a lot of time when the collected blood was left isolated. I offered to help cart the fridge down to the lift. I managed to slip my hand in and grab what I could. I knew one bag would be enough. It was, I must admit, a bit of a lottery, as I knew the bag I picked was consigning the donor to death.'

'What are you talking about? You set this up today?' Tawtridge exclaims.

'Then came the easy part - convincing that jumped-up, self-aggrandizing waste of oxygen I share a cell with, that he had a problem with Quince and that Quince had a problem with him.'

Tawtridge stares goggle-eyed, all too aware that the ecosystem he has set up in here has been played like a fiddle.

'I talked him through the whole damn thing. I even picked where he was to stick him, because you and I both know that's the only place in that entire room the cameras don't cover fully. There's a 7 foot square in the corner that they miss. I assume you know that.'

Tawtridge doesn't answer, words again pointless. He doesn't like where this is going.

'To summarize what I have arranged, a duffle-bag has left the prison today, en route to Greater Manchester Police's Superintendent's office. In that duffle-bag is 5 guard uniforms from your prison coated in Quince's blood. Your CCTV footage will show Quince entering the room, then your guards rushing towards the corner of the room where Quince was standing, a riot, then presumably him being carried out, bleeding to death. I promise you - it won't look good. It will bring a thousand microscopes over every aspect of your reign here, scrutinizing you for the egomaniacal tyrant you are. What do you think they'll find? My guess would be, *a lot*. But I have a lifeline for you. You march me to the front door now, send me on my way, and I will stop the bag from reaching it's destination. Your reputation would be safe.'

Tawtridge is amazed at this. The outrageous bottle of this man to attempt ousting him, and to force him into a corner. The intricacies of the plan, and then his own recognition that all the pieces mentioned are, in fact, in place.

'But don't think for one minute I won't be watching. I'll be keeping an eye on this place, and if I feel if only just for a second, that you have carried on in the same way, with a scant disregard for the justice you have sworn to uphold, I will bring it all down - the good thing about my little safety net is that that evidence is bound forever. There is forever concrete evidence that, presented in the right light, your guards killed a prisoner on your watch. You change your ways and let me go right now, it never has to see the light of day - I'll stop it from reaching it's destination.'

Tawtridge is forced to think about this very carefully, but he has room for one last attempt at bravado. 'This is bullshit. A last ditch ploy from a convicted murderer to run like the twisted weasel he hopes he is trying not to be anymore.'

Ben reaches into his pocket and tosses an object to Tawtridge, that catches the light as it spins through the air. Tawtridge catches it, and holds it up. It is a drained, plastic blood bag, empty save for a few traces of bubbled crimson in the corners. It is labelled in black marker pen 'Richard Quincey, type A+'. Tawtridge stands dumbfounded.

'Do you really want to take the chance that everything I'm saying is made up?' Ben asks.

Tawtridge can't bring himself to say anything. He just stands there staring at Ben, as his expression transforms from vehement anger to disbelieving panic.

6

Against all the limits of his expectation, Ben finds himself massively surprised by what happens next. Tawtridge reassembles himself from the frenzied blancmange he had devolved to on hearing Ben's plan, and silently opens the door to the office.

He marches Ben along the dank corridors and down - all the while the bowels of the prison screaming bloody conflict. A riot is breaking out, escalating in scale with each passing moment. The guttural rumblings combined with Tawtridge's submission echoes eerily symbolic to Ben. He relishes this moment - drinks it in - and, while he is far from home and dry, he is well on the way.

The corridors are still bare, and transmit the echoing ruckus well. Ben imagines that gunshots will soon follow, and wonders whether, if they have to, they will call the police or not, or bring in extra security. That would only bring outside eyes into the prison, and extra scrutiny on Tawtridge's little kingdom. No, Ben thinks - he's going to have to clear this one up all by himself. And what a mess Ben has left him.

'I don't care how you square it away. Or what you do with Quince. Nobody is coming to look for me for the next 15 years, so with your age you can probably leave my absence for the next administration to fathom. Either way, you need to do some covering up. I would imagine that telling the authorities I escaped would only result in questions regarding the security here, and checks and balances will have to be made. I assume you don't fancy that, so I'd advice you let the outside world believe that Ben Bracken is happily holed up in his cell. But think on. Everything you do from here on in... if you don't think I'd approve, then don't do it. Because I will bring this place down without a moments warning if I think you are taking the piss'.

Tawtridge nods once as he walks, his loyal acquiescence assured. They are ending the corridor to a locked metal gate, which Tawtridge opens swiftly. They drop immediately down a flight of steel stairs, and arrive in a cold entrance area that hosts a grand black wooden door - a remnant of earlier times in the prison's lifetime but no less imposing. A guard pokes his head out of a glowing side room, confusion spattered across his face.

'If you want to keep your job, you'll ignore this' Tawtridge yells to him, and the guard's head vanishes immediately like a spooked gopher. 'And you'll open the door.'

Tawtridge and Ben pause by the door, but only momentarily, as an urgent buzzer sounds softly and a lock clunks undone. Tawtridge opens the door immediately, but Ben stops him.

'Harry - you don't really expect me to leave wearing this do you?' Ben says, motioning to his prison issues.

Tawtridge stands dumfounded for a moment.

'I'll need your suit', Ben commands.

Tawtridge stares at Ben in outrage but he knows that Ben holds all the cards - and then some. He has no option at this stage but to play along, and as he strips down to his obese pink belly, y-fronts and pringle socks, he knows his embarrassment is complete. He has been well and truly beaten.

Ben throws on the shirt, trousers and jacket in a flurry, euphemistically holding his nose at the stale sweat stink that hovers on the surface of the clothes. Better than nothing, he grimaces. He knows freedom is mere seconds away - so close to this plan coming off better than he ever could have guessed. He had contingencies, but they were so minor, and they all were pretty last ditch in the grand scheme of things. A future looms large ahead of him, and with it a typhoon, brewing, sure and unstoppable. He is elated, buoyed by the second chance to do good which he has generated for himself. He swears he will not make the same mistakes, and will make the most of this welcome opportunity.

He tosses the prison issues to Tawtridge, who stands there pathetic, stripped of both his clothes and bravado, right down to his grits. Ben turns to the door, and lets the cool air of outside drift in onto his face. It feels damn good.

'I'm a man of my word, Harry' Ben says, while he surveys the cold blue Manchester outside. 'The duffle bag is safe for now.'

'I don't doubt it', Tawtridge says, pulling on the prison issue sweatshirt.

Ben steps through the door, into the cold wet street. Out. Free. Home. Ben takes a second, as the door thunks shut behind him. The suit fits horribly, hanging off his shoulders and down over him like an apron. He simply stands in the street, enjoying the moment. He looks back up at the stone beast that is Strangeways. Silence. You'd never know it was there, or what was going on inside. The ecology that is trying to find it's new balance through bloodshed. Ben takes a step forward, and crosses the street, about to make the short walk into the city centre, and the first steps to redemption.

FOLLOW BEN BRACKEN ONLINE

Twitter: @IAmBenBracken

Web: www.whoisbenbracken.com and
www.benbrackenblog.com

FOLLOW ROBERT PARKER ONLINE

Twitter: @RobertRParker45

Web: www.robertrparker.com

Facebook: www.facebook.com/
robertparkerauthor

NEED MORE BEN BRACKEN?

Visit Robert Parker's Amazon Author Page!

Proof

23241052R00103

Made in the USA
Charleston, SC
15 October 2013